"I'm beginning to think I'd do just about anything for you. Which makes you a dangerous woman."

"No one ever called me dangerous before."

"You don't have a clue..."

Was he feeding her a line?

She knew she was attractive in a casual, understated way. The male sex responded to her. But she was no femme fatale luring unsuspecting men into reckless behavior.

Still, she wanted to believe him, wanted to believe that he felt the same urgent pull she did. Pheromones were a powerful thing.

With reluctance, she made herself step back. "Good night, Carter."

His eyes glittered. "Good night, Abby."

Turning her back on him as she walked away felt risky, but she had to get inside.

She felt his gaze on her back as she headed for the double doors.

She wanted badly to turn around. But she kept on walking...

* * *

Texas Tough by Janice Maynard is part of the Texas Cattleman's Club: Heir Apparent series.

Dear Reader,

Thanks for buying a copy of *Texas Tough*. We may not all live in Texas, but we've certainly had to be tough this past year. I hope you and your families are well and that you are looking forward to better times ahead.

May the summer be filled with sunshine and possibilities!

I'm grateful for each of you...

Fondly,

Janice Maynard

JANICE MAYNARD

TEXAS TOUGH

Special thanks and acknowledgment are given to
Janice Maynard for her contribution to the
Texas Cattleman's Club: Heir Apparent miniseries.

Recycling programs
for this product may
not exist in your area.

ISBN-13: 978-1-335-23294-6

Texas Tough

Copyright © 2021 by Harlequin Books S.A.

This edition published by arrangement with Harlequin Books S.A.

For questions and comments about the quality of this book,
please contact us at CustomerService@Harlequin.com.

Harlequin Enterprises ULC
22 Adelaide St. West, 40th Floor
Toronto, Ontario M5H 4E3, Canada
www.Harlequin.com

Printed in U.S.A.

USA TODAY bestselling author **Janice Maynard** loved books and writing even as a child. After multiple rejections, she finally sold her first manuscript! Since then, she has written sixty books and novellas. Janice lives in Tennessee with her husband, Charles. They love hiking, traveling and family time.

You can connect with Janice at www.janicemaynard.com, www.Twitter.com/janicemaynard, www.Facebook.com/janicemaynardauthor, www.Facebook.com/janicesmaynard and www.Instagram.com/therealjanicemaynard.

Books by Janice Maynard

Harlequin Desire

Southern Secrets

Blame It On Christmas
A Contract Seduction
Bombshell for the Black Sheep

The Men of Stone River

After Hours Seduction
Upstairs Downstairs Temptation
Secrets of a Playboy

Texas Cattleman's Club: Heir Apparent

Texas Tough

Visit her Author Profile page at Harlequin.com, or janicemaynard.com, for more titles.

You can also find Janice Maynard on Facebook, along with other Harlequin Desire authors, at Facebook.com/harlequindesireauthors!

To "romance lovers" everywhere.
You help keep the human spirit alive.
Thanks for your support of the genre and
your dedication to characters and stories.
There would be no books without you!

One

Abby Carmichael was a Starbucks and bright-city-lights kind of girl. What was she doing out here in this godforsaken section of Texas? Maverick County was flat. So flat. And the town of Royal, though charming enough with its wealthy ranchers and rough-edged cowboys, didn't even *have* a storefront for her usual caffeine fix.

So far, she'd been in Royal less than a day, and already she was regretting her current life choice. That was the trouble with being a documentary filmmaker. You had to go where the stories took you. Unfortunately, this particular assignment was smack-dab in the middle of the old Western movies her grandpa used to make her watch.

She pulled off onto a small gravel side road, dazzled by the glorious sunset despite her cranky mood. Flying did that to her. Not to mention having to drive a rental car where all the buttons and knobs were in different places.

Taking a deep breath, she concentrated on losing herself in the moment. All she needed was a hot bath and a good night's sleep. Then she'd be good as new.

Grudgingly, she admired the stunning display of colors painting the evening sky. The orangey reds and golds caught the tips of prairie grasses and made them flame with faux fire. New York City *had* sunsets, but not like this.

While she watched the show, she lowered the car windows. It was June, and plenty humid. The air felt like a blanket, dampening the back of her neck.

At least the heat didn't bother her. Gradually, the peaceful scene smoothed her ragged edges. She'd left her cameras back at the hotel. This excursion was about relaxation and mental health, not work.

Suddenly, she noticed a lone figure far-off on the horizon, silhouetted against the glow of the quickly plummeting sun. The phantom drew closer, taking on shape and form, moving fast, paralleling the road. It was a rider, a horseman. With the sun in her eyes, Abby could make out nothing about the cowboy's features, but she was struck by the grace of man and beast and by the beauty of day's end.

As the horse drew closer, Abby could hear the distinctive *thud, ka-thud* of hooves striking the raw dirt. Something inside her quivered in anticipation.

Grabbing her phone, she jumped out of the car, ran

down the road to get closer and began videoing with her cell. That was often how she processed information. Give her a lens, even a phone lens, and she was happy.

The man's posture was regal, yet easy in the saddle. As if he and the animal were one. Soon, they would be past her.

But without warning, the rider pulled on the reins abruptly. The horse whinnied in protest, reared on its hind legs and settled into a restless halt.

A deep, masculine voice called out across the distance, "You're on private property. Can I help you?"

For the first time, it occurred to Abby that she was entirely alone and far from civilization. *Vulnerable.* A frisson of caution slid down her spine, and some atavistic instinct told her to run. "I have Mace," she warned over her shoulder as she walked rapidly back toward her car.

The man's laugh, a sexy amused chuckle, carried on the breeze. "Mace is good, but it's no match for a Texas shotgun."

Her heart bobbled in her chest, her breath hitching as she moved faster and faster away from him. She had come farther than she realized. Surely, the man was joking. But she didn't plan on finding out.

She jumped into her car, executed a flawless U-turn and gunned the engine, heading back toward town.

Two hours later, Abby was still a bit shaky. Her room felt claustrophobic, so she grabbed her billfold, pocketed her key card and went downstairs. Maybe a drink would calm her nerves. She wasn't normally so skittish, but everything about this place felt alien.

Not the hotel. The Miramar was lovely. Comfortable. Just the right amount of pampered luxury. And still in her budget. She *could* have stayed at the lavish Bellamy, but Royal's premier five-star resort was too high-profile for her needs.

At the entrance to the bar, she paused and took a breath, soothed by the dim lights and the traditional furnishings. The room was filled with lots of brass and candles and fresh flowers. And almost *no* people. The bartender looked up when she walked in. He was an older man with graying hair and a craggy face. "Plenty of room at the bar," he said. "As you can see. But feel free to take a booth if you'd prefer."

"Thanks." Abby debated briefly, then sat down at the booth in the corner. It was private, and she felt the need to regroup. She was well able to handle herself in public, or even wave off the occasional pushy male. After all, she was a New Yorker. But tonight, she just wanted to unwind.

The bartender came around to her table, pad in hand. "What can I get you, young lady? The appetizers are on that card right there."

She smiled at him. "No food for me, thanks. But a glass of zinfandel, please. Beringer if you have it."

"Yes, ma'am," he said, walking away to fill her order.

When the man returned with her drink, Abby took the glass with a muttered thanks. "I needed this," she confessed. "I was driving outside of town, and some macho cowboy on a horse threatened me with a shot-gun. It was scary."

The bartender raised a skeptical eyebrow. "Doesn't sound like Royal. Folks around here are pretty hospitable as a rule."

"Maybe," Abby said, unconvinced.

When the man frowned and walked away, she realized belatedly that either she had insulted his fellow Texans, or maybe he thought she was an interloper dressed a tad too casually for the Miramar. Whenever she flew, she liked to be comfortable. Today, she had worn a thin flannel shirt over a silky camisole with her oldest, softest jeans and ankle boots.

Oh, well, it was late, and the bar was almost empty. She hoped no one would even notice her...

Carter Crane yawned and stretched as he sauntered into the Miramar and headed for the bar. He should be on his way home for a good night's sleep, but he had just finished a late evening meeting with a breeder, and he was feeling restless for no good reason he could pinpoint.

At thirty-four, he'd thought he would have a wife and maybe a kid by now. But he had gambled on the wrong woman and lost. His fault. He should have seen it coming.

The gorgeous summer weather made him feel more alone than usual. Maybe because this was the time of year for socializing. Carter hadn't *socialized* with a woman in far too long. A year—or maybe a year and a half?

He worked hard enough to keep his reckless impulses in check. Mostly.

Tonight, he felt the sting.

There were other more popular watering holes in Royal, but he liked the private, laid-back ambience at the Miramar.

He grinned at the bartender. "Hey, Sam. I'll have a beer, please. The usual." Carter's dad had known Sam since the two men were boys. Now his father was enjoying the good life in a fancy condo on Miami Beach.

Sam brought the frothy beer and set it on a napkin. "Food?"

"Nope. I'm good."

"How's the herd?" the older man asked.

"Best one yet. Barring tornadoes or droughts, we should have a banner year."

"Your dad says you work too hard."

"It's all I know how to do," Carter said. "Besides, he was the same way."

Sam nodded as he rinsed glasses and hung them overhead. "True. But not now. He misses you."

"I didn't realize you kept in touch."

"Now and then," Sam said.

Carter changed the subject. "You won't believe what happened to me earlier tonight. Some crazy tourist lady threatened me with Mace. On my own property."

"How do you know she was a tourist?"

"Who else would carry Mace?" Carter scoffed. "Royal is a safe town."

"Maybe she didn't know that. And the way *I* heard it, you threatened her with a shotgun."

He gaped. "Say what?"

Sam pointed. "Little gal's over there. You probably should apologize. It rattled her."

Carter glanced over his shoulder. "Looks like she enjoys being alone."

The bartender shook his head, eyes dancing. "Come on. I'll introduce you, so she won't think you're hitting on her."

Sam didn't wait. He poured a glass of wine, swung around the end of the bar and went to where the woman sat, half shielded by the high wooden back of the banquette. "This one's on the house, ma'am. And I'd like to introduce you to Carter Crane. He's one of Royal's fine, upstanding citizens. I think he has something to say to you."

Carter felt his neck get hot. The woman eyeing him warily was visibly skeptical of Sam's assessment. "May I sit for a moment?" he asked.

After a long hesitation, the woman nodded. "Help yourself."

He eased into the booth, beer in hand, and cut to the chase. "I was the one you saw on the road outside of town. I was kidding about the shotgun," he said quickly as her eyes rounded. "It was a joke."

The woman looked him over, not saying a word. Though her perusal wasn't entirely comfortable, Carter seized on the excuse to do his own inventory. She was slim and young, almost too young to be drinking alcohol, but maybe her looks were deceptive.

Her hair was long and brown and wavy, her eyes a rich brown to match. She wasn't wearing a speck of makeup, except possibly mascara. Even then, her lush lashes *could* be real, he supposed.

It was her complexion, however, that elevated her from merely pretty to gorgeous. Light brown with a hint of sunlight, her skin was glowing and perfect.

Carter felt a stirring of lust and was taken aback. Ordinarily, he preferred his women sophisticated and worldly. This artless, unadorned female was the rose that didn't need gilding. She was *stunning*.

He cleared his throat. "As Sam said, I'm Carter Crane. I own the Sunset Acres ranch. Most days I'm proud of it. Others, I curse it. What's your name?"

The tiniest of smiles tilted her lips. "Abby Carmichael. And I knew you were kidding about the shotgun."

"No, you didn't." He chuckled. "I've never seen a woman move so fast."

She lifted her chin. "I was in a hurry to get back to the hotel, because I needed to pee. It had nothing to do with you."

He laughed again, letting the blatant lie go unchallenged, charmed by her voice and her wide-eyed appeal. "I think I recognize the accent," he said. "You're from back East, right? New York? My college roommate was born and bred in Manhattan."

"I don't have an accent," she insisted. "You're the one with the drawl."

Carter shook his head slowly. "I never argue with a lady," he said.

"Why do I not believe that?"

Her wry sarcasm made him grin all over again. She

might be young, but she was no naive kid. "What brings you to Royal?" he asked.

"I'm doing a documentary on the festival—Soiree on the Bay."

He grimaced. "Ah."

She cocked her head. "You don't approve?"

"I don't *not* approve," he answered carefully. "But events like that bring hordes of outsiders into town. I like my space and my privacy."

"The festival takes place on Appaloosa Island."

"Doesn't matter. People have to sleep and eat and shop. Royal will be a madhouse."

"You're awfully young to be a curmudgeon. How old are you, forty?"

He sat up straighter, affronted. "I'm thirty-four, for your information. And even a *young* man can have strong opinions."

"True…"

From the twinkle in her eye, he saw that she had been baiting him. "Very funny," he muttered. "But since we've broached the subject, how old are you? I guessed seventeen at first, but you're drinking wine, so I don't know."

"Didn't your mother tell you never to ask a woman her age?"

"Seventeen it is."

"Don't be insulting. I'm twenty-four. Plenty old enough to recognize a man with an agenda."

"Hey," he protested, holding up his hands. "I only came over to say hello. And to assure you that you're in no danger here in Royal."

"I can handle myself, Mr. Crane."

"Carter," he insisted.

"Carter. And because I'm a nice person, I'll forgive you for the shotgun incident, if you'll do me a favor."

He bristled. "There *was* no shotgun incident, woman." Was she flirting with him? Surely not.

She smiled broadly now. The wattage of that smile kicked him in the chest like a mule. "If you say so…"

"What kind of favor?" He wasn't born yesterday and wasn't going to give her carte blanche.

"A simple one. I'd like to see your ranch. Film it. And interview you. On camera."

"Why?" He was naturally suspicious. Life had taught him that things weren't always what they seemed. "I have nothing at all to do with the festival. I don't even care about it. Period."

She shrugged. When she did, one shoulder of her shirt slipped, revealing the strap of her camisole and more of her smooth skin. His chest tightened as did parts south.

The fact that her expression was matter-of-fact didn't jibe with his racing pulse.

"My documentary about the festival will be punctuated by scenes from around Royal. To provide local color. Since Royal is home to the famed Texas Cattleman's Club, it only makes sense for me to include ranching. You're the only rancher I know, so here we are."

"My days are busy," he muttered, sounding pedantic, even to his own ears. "I don't have time for futzing around with movie stuff."

Her jaw dropped. "Do you have any idea how patronizing you sound? My job is no less important than yours, Mr. Carter Crane. But don't worry. I'm sure I can find another rancher to show me the ropes."

Like hell you will. The visceral response told him he was wading into deep water. "Fine. I'll do it," he said, trying not to sound as grumpy as he felt. This artless, beautiful young woman was throwing him off his game. "Give me your contact info."

Abby reached into her wallet and extracted a business card. It was stylish, but casual. Much like the gal with her hand extended. He reached out and took the small rectangle, perusing it. "I'll call you," he said.

"That's what they all say," she deadpanned.

"I said I would, and I will."

"I appreciate it, Carter."

The way she said his name, two distinct syllables with a feminine nuance, made him itchy. Suddenly, he was in no great hurry to head home.

"I could stay a little longer," he said. "Since you're new in town."

The rosy tint on her cheekbones deepened. "How chivalrous."

"May I buy you another glass of wine?"

The woman shook her head. "I'm a lightweight. But I wouldn't say no to a Coke and nachos. Though this place might be too upscale for comfort food."

"I'm sure Sam will rustle some up for us," he told her.

"I love how you do that."

Carter frowned. "Do what?"

"Talk like a cowboy. *Rustle some up.*"

He leaned back in the booth, feeling some of the day's stress melt away. This unexpected encounter was the most fun he'd had in ages. Though he was likely destined for a cold shower and a restless night. "Are you making fun of me, Ms. Carmichael?"

"You can call me Abby," she said.

"Don't move…" He went to the bar, gave Sam their order and came back. "I told him we wanted fried pickles, too."

His companion wrinkled her nose. "Ew, gross. Don't you care about your health?"

Carter hid a smile as he took off the noose around his neck. He removed his jacket, too, and stretched his arms over his head, yawning. "Do I look unhealthy to you?"

Two

Not fair, Carter Crane. Abby would have choked on her pickle… If she'd been eating one. Which she wasn't. Her face heated and her pulse stumbled as she drank him in from head to toe. The man was eye candy, leading man material, drop-dead *gorgeous*.

Carter Crane was a lot of male. In every way. When she had seen him earlier on horseback, she'd barely had the time to digest what he looked like, much less what he was wearing. But she was pretty sure it hadn't been this expensive navy sport coat, pristine white button-down and tailored dress pants. Not to mention the patterned crimson necktie that he had shed so quickly.

The fact that he managed to wear cowboy boots without looking even a smidge ridiculous told her he was the real deal.

Underneath the soft cotton fabric of his shirt was a chest that went on for miles. Hard, with ripped abs. She'd bet her gym membership on it.

Summer-morning blue eyes were bracketed with tiny lines from squinting into the sun. His hair was brown and tousled, as if he had just tumbled out of bed and run his hands through the silky strands.

She downed a gulp of the Coke that Sam had just set on the table. "I have no medical training," she said primly. "You might be at death's door for all I know." When she thought her expression wouldn't give her away, she sat back and gave him an even stare. "I'm not a doctor, but you look fine to me."

He raised an eyebrow. "*Fine?* That's the best you can do?"

Humor lifted the corners of her lips, despite her best efforts to take him down a peg or two. "You know what you look like, rancher man. You don't need me to stroke your ego or anything else."

Carter blinked and quirked a brow. "Umm…"

Suddenly, she heard the blatantly suggestive comment she had made. Unwittingly, but still… "Moving on," she said briskly, trying to pretend she was not embarrassed. Or interested. Or *turned on*.

Her companion didn't call her out on her faux pas. Instead, he leaned forward on his elbows and offered her a pickle. "You're a filmmaker. Surely you sample the local cuisine when you travel. Come on, Abby. At least try one."

Against her better judgment, she opened her lips and let him tuck the crispy slice in between. She bit down automatically and felt the flavors explode on her tongue. The sharp bite of the pickle and the tangy seasoning of the outer layer were utterly divine. "Oh, my… this is good."

Carter sprawled in the corner of the booth and scooped up two for his own pleasure. "Told you," he said as he chewed and swallowed.

Abby was mesmerized by the ripples in his tanned throat. She turned to the nachos in desperation. Apparently, New York wasn't the only place in the world with good food. "These are amazing, too."

Carter offered her a napkin, his gaze intense. "You have cheese on your chin," he told her quietly.

Abby quaked inside. This was getting way too personal, way too fast. She needed to put on the brakes. "Tell me about your family." She blurted out the request.

Carter ran a hand across the back of his neck, eyeing her with undisguised male interest. Abby was interested, too, but they had just met, and she certainly wasn't going to invite him upstairs to her hotel room.

Finally, he sighed. "Not much to tell. I'm the older of two kids. One sister. My parents retired to Florida, leaving me in charge of the ranch. It's been in our family for five generations. Sunset Acres is not only in my blood, it's part of me."

A squiggle of disappointment settled in Abby's stomach. The last thing she needed was to get involved with a man who was wedded to a plot of dirt in this remote, flat, rural landscape. "Did you always want to be a rancher?"

He shook his head slowly. "When I was ten, I wanted to be an astronaut."

"Seriously? Wow. That's cool. Why didn't you go that route?"

"Several reasons. Turns out, I'm claustrophobic. But more to the point, one of my ancestors fought with Davy Crockett at the Alamo. Walking away from a couple centuries of family history wasn't an option." He signaled Sam for another round of drinks.

They were the only customers in the bar now. Abby glanced at her watch. "Should we go? Maybe Sam wants to shut down."

Carter shook his head slowly, his gaze still focused on her mouth. "We have another hour," he said.

Those four words were innocuous, but the handsome rancher's tone was not. Suddenly, Abby wanted to take off her shirt. She was far too hot. The camisole was not indecent. But such a move might signal something she wasn't ready to signal.

"What shall we talk about?" she asked in desperation, her hormones melting into a puddle of heated sexual attraction. "Politics? Religion. Something easy?"

Carter leaned forward and touched the fingernail on her pinkie, barely any contact at all. "I want to talk about you."

Carter wasn't the kind of man to press a female who wasn't interested. He'd been taught by his daddy to respect the fairer sex. And truth be told, women usually came on to him, not the other way around.

If Abby had been uninterested, he would have paid

the check and walked out of the bar. But she *was* interested. He'd bet his prize stallion on it.

Still, he gave her an out. "Should I go now?" he asked gruffly. "Am I making you uncomfortable?"

She stared at him, pupils dilated slightly, as he rubbed her fingernail. He'd never done such a thing before. Ever. In fact, in the cold light of day, this move on his part would probably look dorky and dumb.

But right now, they were connected.

Her chest rose and fell. "No," she whispered. "Don't go."

His hand shook. So much so, that he pulled it back and tucked it under the table out of sight. It wouldn't be good for her to realize how close he was to begging for a night in her bed.

One-night stands were indulgences he had given up long ago—about the time his father began handing over more and more responsibility for the ranch. Carter was not a selfish twentysomething anymore. He was a landowner, a wealthy rancher and a respected member of the community.

For Abby Carmichael, though, he might make an exception.

He cleared his throat, trying to focus on anything other than the fantasy swirling in his head. "As I recall, you never answered my question about where you're from."

"You were right about that. New York City. I went to film school at New York University, and I still live with my mom when I'm in town. Apartments are ridiculously expensive."

"So I've heard. NYU. I'm impressed. Isn't it hard to get accepted?"

She grimaced. "Definitely. But I had two things going in my favor. My father is Black, and my mom is white, so I ticked the biracial box."

"And the other?" he asked.

"Daddy is a filmmaker out on the West Coast. He and my mom are divorced. I spent summers with him growing up and got the movie bug. He asked a couple of his influential friends to write recommendation letters for me. So here I am," she explained.

"Why documentaries?"

"We're a visual society. As much as I love books and believe in the power of the written word, there's no faster way to touch someone's heart or change someone's opinion than with a well-framed documentary." She spoke with intensity.

"What piqued your interest about Soiree on the Bay?"

"Well, you talked about family legacy—" She smiled, her face lighting up. "I can claim one, as well, though not so long-lived. My grandmother was at Woodstock. In fact, she supposedly got pregnant with my mother there. Gave birth to her when she was barely eighteen. Music is in my blood, and in any big gathering like that, there are fascinating stories to tell. Lots of stories. I want to capture this festival from beginning to end."

Carter had lost his appetite for nachos and fried pickles. What he wanted now, *needed* now, was far more visceral. "I love your passion," he said slowly. "I'm sure that comes across in your work."

Pink stained her cheeks again. "I hope so. And you'll let me film you? Please?"

With Abby's big brown eyes staring at him hopefully, he felt churlish for turning her down. But he sensed that a yes from him right now would ensnare him in something he wasn't sure he was prepared for, neither the movie project nor the woman who wasn't going to stick around.

"I'll think about it. I promise."

He saw her disappointment, but he held firm.

"Well, thank you then," she said. "For the nachos and Cokes. And the conversation. But I should get some sleep. The time change is hitting me." She yawned, proving her point.

They both slid out of the booth at the same time, suddenly standing far too close. Carter's throat constricted. He wanted to grab her up and kiss her until her body went limp with pleasure.

He shoved his hands in his pockets. "Welcome to Royal, Abby Carmichael. I hope you enjoy all we have to offer..."

Abby left the cowboy standing in the bar, his hot gaze giving her second and third thoughts about being reckless. It wasn't vanity on her part to think he would have accompanied her upstairs. There were enough sparks arcing between them to pretty much guarantee the sex would be explosive.

But once she was in her room, she knew she had done the right thing. She was really tired, and she had a meeting tomorrow that was very important. Lila Jones, from Royal's Chamber of Commerce, was going to welcome her to town and even give her a tour of Appaloosa Island.

Abby hoped she would also be able to do some preliminary filming.

As she showered and crawled into bed, however, it was hard to keep her mind on work. When she closed her eyes, Carter Crane was there with her, laughing, flirting, teasing. It had been a long time since she had met someone so intriguing, so different from the men she knew in New York. Or even California for that matter.

Carter was his own man. A Texas rancher. That meant something in this part of the world. Still, even aside from his ranching expertise and land holdings, she knew he would stand out anywhere in the country. Carter had a commanding presence, an innate confidence that was very appealing and sexy. And though his intense masculinity was flavored with a tinge of arrogance, the arrogance wasn't off-putting.

After the *interesting* evening she'd had with him— starting out on a deserted stretch of highway and ending in a dimly lit bar—she might have tossed and turned. Fortunately, exhaustion claimed her, and she slept long and deeply.

When she awoke the next morning at 6:00 a.m., her batteries were recharged, and she was eager to jumpstart her day. After heading out for a run and then taking a quick shower, she couldn't deny feeling bummed when she glanced at her phone. Not a single text or missed call. Would Carter agree to let her film him?

He had promised to think about it. But without a time frame. He might keep her dangling indefinitely.

She would give him forty-eight hours. After that, she would assume his answer was no. Which meant she would have to find someone else. Handsome ranchers might be a dime a dozen in this part of the world. Who knew?

When she stood at the window for a moment and looked out over the heart of Royal, she had to admit it wasn't so bad after all. Though it wasn't quite big enough to be called a city by her standards, it was definitely a very nice, large town. The broad main thoroughfare was landscaped with flowers and ornamental trees, and in the distance, she could make out the shape of the venerable Texas Cattleman's Club.

There were clothing stores and restaurants, bars and banks—even an intentionally retro country emporium. In her research, she had learned that the schools were rated highly, and in addition to all the wealthy cattle barons, the town was home to artists and potters and other creative types.

It wasn't New York City or Malibu, but she could see the appeal.

A tiny alarm beeped on her watch.

Grabbing up her roomy leather tote, a water bottle and a rain jacket just in case, she headed out to meet her tour guide.

Lila was right on time, waiting at the curb in front of the hotel. She jumped out of her car. "It's wonderful to see you again, Abby. Welcome to Royal."

Abby shook the other woman's hand. "Thanks. I'm

happy to be here." As they got settled, she took stock of her companion. She had met the other woman in LA and knew she was about her age, maybe a little older. She reminded Abby of the actress Zooey Deschanel.

Lila waved at the back seat. "I have snacks when you get hungry."

"Thanks. I appreciate your taking me out to the island today. But tell me again why I can't just stay there for the length of my project?" This was going to be a heck of a commute. Three hours each way.

Lila chuckled. "Well, first of all, you have to get used to Texas. Everything is big out here in the Lone Star State. Big ranches, big egos, big open spaces. It's fairly common to travel by helicopter or small plane. You'll find landing strips just about anywhere you want to go."

"But I can't stay on the island?"

"Not realistically. It doesn't have everyday amenities. There are some huge mansions out on the western end, but the rest of it is undeveloped. That's why the Edmond family decided it would be the perfect spot for Soiree on the Bay."

"And Mustang Point?"

"Mostly private residences for the super wealthy. Mustang has a ton of water sports, but I promise you, living in Royal while you do this project will be far more reasonable. Not to mention the fact that all the people you'll need to interview for your documentary live in Royal or just outside of town."

They had been driving for twenty minutes when Lila pulled the car into a gravel parking lot. Abby's stomach pitched. She was a frequent flier on coast-to-coast routes. But the tiny prop plane sitting on the narrow strip of tarmac looked flimsy and unimpressive.

Lila didn't seem at all concerned. She hopped out and greeted the young pilot. "Hi, Danny. Thanks for running us out to the Point."

The freckled kid ducked his head bashfully. "Happy to do it, Miss Lila. I need flying hours to keep my license up-to-date, and Daddy said not to charge you a dime."

"I'll add my thanks, too," Abby said.

Soon, they were airborne. Abby took out her camera and aimed through the tiny plane window. The result was not great, but it helped her get a feel for the landscape.

Lila watched with interest. "What kind of camera are you using? It looks fairly portable and light."

Abby sat back in her seat. "Twelve pounds. It's a Panasonic DVX200. Pricey, but it shoots great 4K resolution and has up to twelve stops of dynamic range."

"I'll pretend I know what you're talking about," Lila said, laughing.

"The camera was a gift from my dad when I graduated. He was really hoping I would follow in his footsteps."

"And now here you are."

"Yes. After you invited me to film the festival, Dad hooked me up with somebody at Netflix who might be interested in a documentary about Soiree on the Bay, but I'll have to find a strong human interest angle."

"A hook as they say?"

"Exactly." Abby tucked her camera back in her bag.

Incorporating Carter's story would add depth and local color, but she wasn't holding her breath. "What's on our schedule for today?"

Lila tapped her phone and perused what was clearly a calendar. "We'll catch the ferry out to Appaloosa Island. It's a quick, fifteen-minute ride. On the island, Jerome will meet us. He acts as a groundskeeper for several of the landowners, and he's arranged for me—and by extension you—to have the use of a golf cart anytime you come out to the island. You'll just call him in advance, and it will be waiting. Today, we'll do an informal tour and answer any questions you might have."

"I really appreciate you giving up a huge part of your morning and afternoon to do this."

"No problem. It's my job, of course. And besides, any chance to get out of the office is a plus."

As the small plane touched down, Abby glanced at her watch. The trip had taken an hour and a half. So, better than the three-hour drive she'd been expecting, but still not quick. She was going to have to be very disciplined about planning her shooting schedule. Much of the groundwork would have to be done in Royal.

She grabbed her things, thanked the young pilot and followed the other woman out of the plane. The ferry dock was a quarter-mile walk. Though a small line of cars sat waiting to cross, foot traffic was almost nonexistent. Abby and Lila boarded and made their way inside the air-conditioned cabin.

Abby frowned as she thought about the logistics. "How is this going to work during the actual festival?"

Lila uncapped her water bottle and took a sip. "It

won't be easy. The organizers are planning to add four more ferries. And parking on the island will be limited. Festivalgoers who want to have their personal vehicles on-site will pay a hefty premium in addition to their ticket price."

"So part of the cachet of the festival will be that it's hard to access…it's *exclusive*."

"Exactly."

At the end of the brief ferry ride, Lila waved at an older man with deeply tanned skin and grizzled salt-and-pepper hair. *That must be Jerome*, Abby guessed. He sat in one golf cart alongside a second cart with a much younger driver.

The younger man jumped down and slid onto the seat beside Jerome. The groundskeeper tipped his hat. "That one's all yours, Ms. Lila. When you ladies are done for the day, just park it right here and leave the keys under the seat."

Abby's eyes widened. "Isn't that dangerous?"

The other three chuckled. "Safe as going to church," Jerome said. "You little gals have fun."

Lila motioned toward the back of the golf cart. "Toss your things in there and hang on. Not everything has been paved yet."

The sun was hot and directly overhead, but a breeze danced off the water. Trinity Bay was idyllic, deep blue, touched with whitecaps. No wonder the Edmonds had acquired this private island. It was exquisite.

Abby looked around with interest as the small vehicle lurched into motion. The festival grounds were larger than she had imagined. And far more upscale.

This would be no Woodstock with music lovers lounging on the grass.

Lila narrated as they wound among the structures that smelled of new wood and excitement. "The two main stages will anchor the event with headliners. Big names. Crowd-pleasers. The scattering of smaller venues you see will be home to quirkier bands. The kind of musical groups that in five years might become household names."

"And over there across the main pathway?" Abby curled her fingers around the top edge of the golf cart. Some areas had been prepped for sod, but others were covered in wood chips. The golf cart bumped and jolted.

"Those are the wine bars and pop-up restaurants. Each will have a celebrity chef."

"Wow." The logistics of putting on an enormous music festival—on an *island*—boggled the mind. There was so much to coordinate: food shipments, the sound equipment, a medical presence, seating—presumably chairs and benches. The portable toilets… Abby definitely wouldn't want to be the person in charge. The whole thing could be a smashing success or a raging headache fraught with disaster.

Lila eased the golf cart onto a small point surrounded by water on two sides. "I brought fruit and cheese. And a bottle of wine. You hungry?"

"Actually, I am."

Lila wasn't a huge talker, which Abby liked. It was peaceful to sit in silence, watch the water and enjoy the simple pleasures of an alfresco meal.

Without warning, a vision of Carter Crane popped

into her head. The handsome rancher was no doubt neck-deep in cattle ranch business in the middle of a busy workday. Maybe Abby could convince him that his routine was exactly what she found fascinating. There was only so much video she could take here on the island before the festival got underway. But to immerse the viewer in the flavor of Texas, she would need solid footage of what it meant to be from Royal.

Lila yawned. "Do you want to get some preliminary shots? I can check email on my phone or maybe grab a quick nap. Take your time."

"That would be great." Abby finished her light lunch and slid out of the golf cart, going around to the back to retrieve her camera. For the actual festival she would need her tripods. Today, though, she wanted to shoot the mood of the unoccupied island.

The bay was an obvious star. Out in the distance, sailboats glided along, pushed by the wind. Abby was sure she saw a dolphin break the surface in a carefree arc. When she had what she wanted from the water, she turned to the land.

Some of the empty structures would be dramatic in black and white. She paused for a moment, listening. Trying to envision what the energy of the crowd would sound like… Imagining the steady thump of the bass. The sharp twang of an electric guitar.

Steadying the camera on her shoulder, she panned from left to right. And caught a cowboy dead in the middle of her viewfinder.

Three

Carter enjoyed catching Abby Carmichael off guard. She had incredible confidence and self-possession for someone so young, but he had managed to rattle her. He saw it in her eyes when she lowered the camera.

"Carter," she said, her gaze wary. "What are you doing here?"

He hid a grin by rubbing his chin. "I was in the neighborhood and thought I'd drop by." He took a moment to enjoy the picture she made. Being a filmmaker was a physically demanding job at times. Abby must have dressed for comfort and professionalism, but her choice of clothing flattered her.

She wore an ankle-length, halter-neck sundress of a thin gauzy material that hinted at the shape of her body. The colorful fabric made him think of Caribbean islands and cold drinks with tiny umbrellas. Abby's beautiful wavy hair was down, despite the heat. The breeze fanned strands out across her golden-skinned shoulders.

She chewed her bottom lip, clearly convinced he was up to no good. Maybe she was right. "We're miles from Royal," she said. "And I have it on good authority that your little cows are a demanding lot."

He laughed softly, suddenly very glad he had come. "None of my cows are little, city girl. Besides, I told them I wanted the day off."

She frowned. "Your cattle?"

"Nope. My staff."

"Oh…" She glanced back over her shoulder. "I should go. Lila will be waiting for me."

He reached for the camera. "Here. I'll carry that. I'd like to say hello."

Abby surrendered the video equipment with obvious reluctance, but she fell into step beside him. "You know Lila?"

"Everybody knows *everybody* in Royal. Besides, Lila is big news lately. She enticed a celebrity Instagram influencer—whatever the hell that is—to come to Royal and promote the music festival. Next thing I knew, the gossip was flying, and Lila was engaged to Zach Benning."

"I've heard about Zach, and I did notice the gorgeous ring on her finger. Sounds like a fairy tale."

Carter grimaced. "Don't tell me you're one of those."

Abby stopped abruptly. "What does that mean?"

He faced her with the camera tucked under his arm. "A dewy-eyed romantic. I thought documentary makers were more realistic." Though he had to admit that her soft brown irises were pretty damn gorgeous. A man could dive into those eyes and get lost.

"You think romantic love is fiction?"

"Yes," he said baldly. Perhaps his response was harsh, but he knew better than most men that romance was little more than a charade.

Abby continued walking, her expression thoughtful. When they approached a golf cart parked by the water, Lila Jones got out and waved. "Hey there, Carter. What brings you to Appaloosa Island? You're several weeks early for the festival."

He kissed her cheek. "You know I'm not a festival kind of guy. But I haven't had a chance to congratulate you on your engagement."

Lila blushed. "Thanks."

Abby studied them both. "How long have you two known each other?"

Carter shrugged. "Forever... Folks in Royal tend to put down roots."

Lila's brows drew together. "I might ask you two the same question. Abby, I thought you only got into town last night."

"That's true. But I went for a drive, and on a dusty secluded road, Carter here threatened to shoot me."

"No, no, *no*," Carter protested. "The truth is, Abby isn't as innocent as she looks. The woman tried to Mace me."

Abby's eyes danced. "I don't think that's a verb."

Lila put her hands on her hips. "I'm missing something."

Carter lifted his face toward the sun, feeling more carefree than he had in a long time. "Let's just say that our first meeting was dramatic and our second far more cordial."

"I need to hear the whole story," Lila insisted.

"I'll fill you in on the way back." Abby took her camera from Carter and tucked it into a cushioned bag. Then she climbed into the cart and glanced over her shoulder at him. "We have to go. Our ride is picking us up in twenty minutes."

Carter lifted a brow, looking at Lila. "Danny getting in practice miles?"

"You bet."

"Abby?" He touched her arm briefly, feeling the insistent *zing* of attraction. "I was hoping I might persuade you to drive back with me. When we get to town, I'll take you to dinner."

"I came with Lila," she said, her face giving nothing away.

Lila shook her head slowly. "Carter has a gorgeous black Porsche. It's by far the better offer."

He smiled at the woman in the passenger seat. "You said you wanted to interview me. Now's your chance."

"I said I wanted to *film* you."

"Yes, but the interview should come first. I've been reading up on how to make a documentary. I wanted to be ready."

Abby's lips parted, almost as if she felt the same magnetic sexual pull and wasn't sure what to do about it. "I don't want to abandon Lila."

Lila pooh-poohed that idea. "Go with Carter. You

and I will have plenty of time together. I don't mind at all. Honestly."

Carter gave both women his most innocent smile. "Abby?"

"Okay, fine." She exited the golf cart with a graceful swish of skirt and a flash of toned thigh. "Let me grab my stuff."

Lila intervened. "Better yet, why don't we just give Carter a ride back to the dock? It's too hot to walk around with no shade."

"I'll take that offer," he said. The golf cart had two rows of seating, so he slid in behind the women. Abby reclaimed her spot in the front. If he leaned forward, he could kiss one of her bare shoulders. That thought had him shifting uncomfortably on the seat. Maybe spending three hours in the car with the delectable filmmaker wasn't such a good idea after all.

He had parked the convertible adjacent to the dock. The ferry was moments away from pulling out. Because there was no room in his small sports car for a second passenger, Lila and Abby exchanged goodbyes, and Lila boarded on foot.

Carter helped Abby in, started the engine and, when instructed, eased his vehicle onto the ramp and into the ferry. Because the ride was so short, they stayed in the car with the windows down. Abby had her camera out shooting the seagulls chasing the boat. He suspected it was a ploy not to have to converse with him.

Was she nervous? Carter wasn't. Well, not exactly. He would describe it as being *on edge*. His senses were heightened, and truth be told, he rarely reacted this strongly to a woman he had just met.

When they reached Mustang Point, Carter and Abby greeted Danny and said goodbye to Lila. Then they wound their way back to the highway. Carter still had the top up. The blistering heat was too much right now.

He adjusted the air and glanced at his silent companion. "You okay?"

Abby smiled, playing with her large hoop earring. "Yes. This is a very nice car."

"I'm glad you like it. When we get closer to Royal, there's a two-lane road that turns off the main drag but still leads into town. It's the old highway actually. I thought we could put the top down then and enjoy the view."

"Sounds good."

Carter gripped the wheel, wondering why he had taken the day off. He never played hooky in the middle of the week. In fact, he had been known to work six and seven days in a row. The pace wasn't healthy, but ranching took up most of his life.

It was just him. All day every day. Carrying the weight of a family legacy. He wasn't complaining. He knew he was lucky beyond measure.

But Abby Carmichael was the best kind of interruption.

"How old were you when your parents divorced?" he asked quietly. His own mom and dad were heading for their forty-seventh anniversary.

Abby sighed. She had kicked off her sandals and was sitting with one leg tucked beneath her. "I was five. So

I don't remember a lot. But as an adult, I finally understood why the marriage unraveled."

"Oh?"

"My mother was an Upper East Side society princess," she explained. "My grandparents owned tons of real estate, and Mom had the best of everything growing up. She met my father during a spring break trip to Jamaica."

"Her parents didn't approve because he wasn't in their social circle?" he mused.

"They probably didn't, but that wasn't the tack they took in opposing the relationship. My father's family was wealthy, too. They were bankers and lawyers in Jamaica. Daddy was a musician when he and Mom met, but he was studying to be a filmmaker. Mom says her parents weren't impressed with the odds of success in that career."

Carter looked over at her before returning his eyes to the road. "Were they right?"

"Yes and no. It took my dad years to break into the industry. And it meant going where the jobs were. If he'd had a wife and kid in tow, it might never have happened."

"Did your grandparents give in?"

"Sadly, no." She sighed. "My mother wanted a cathedral wedding with all the frills. In the end, she had to settle for a Vegas chapel."

"Did her parents ever come around?"

"When she got pregnant with me…yes. But maybe my mom and dad were too different from the beginning. Even sharing a child couldn't keep them together."

"I'm sorry, Abby," he said quietly. "It must be hard to have them on opposite coasts."

When he glanced at her again, she was staring straight ahead, as if the road held answers. Her expression—what he could see of it in a quick glance—was pensive. "I've learned to be happy anywhere. I love both of them, and whatever animosity there might have been during the divorce evaporated over the years."

"Have you thought about where you'll settle? For the long haul?"

She shot him a look of surprise. "I don't know that I *will* settle. Living out of a suitcase doesn't bother me."

"But surely you see yourself putting down roots eventually."

"Maybe."

"Don't you want kids someday?"

"Do *you*?" Her question was sharp. "Why do people ask women that? I bet never once has anyone tried to pin you down on the fatherhood question."

"Well, you'd be wrong then," he said wryly. "My mother brings it up regularly. I'm a terrible disappointment to her. And I have ten years on you, so the pressure is mounting."

"I guess you're glad they don't live here anymore."

"Not really," he said. "I miss them. But they deserve this time to spread their wings. The ranch always tied them down."

Abby heard the clear affection in his voice and experienced the oddest moment of jealousy. She loved her parents—of course she did. And she got along well with both of them. But the three of them weren't a family unit. Not like the close bond Carter evidently had with his mom and dad. Abby and her parents were two halves of a family that somehow didn't add up to a whole.

She let the conversation drop. Carter didn't seem to mind. It was a beautiful day for a drive. In a strange way, she felt very comfortable with him. Well, that was true as long as she ignored the palpable sexual undertones.

Without meaning to, she dozed. When she jerked awake and ran her hands over her face, she was embarrassed. "Sorry," she muttered. "I was sleep-deprived coming into this trip. I guess I'm still catching up."

"No worries. You're cute when you snore."

"I *don't* snore," she retorted, mildly offended, and also worried that he wasn't joking. Carter didn't answer. He kept his eyes on the road, but she could see the smile that curved his lips. The man had great lips. World-class. Perfect for kissing.

To keep herself from fixating on his mouth and his jaw and all the other yummy parts of him, she looked at the view beyond the car windows. Fields and more fields. Cows and more cows. It was all she could see in any direction.

Carter shot her a sideways glance. "What?"

Abby frowned. "I didn't say anything."

"No. But you were thinking really loud. You can say it. You don't like Texas."

It seemed churlish to agree. "That's an overstatement."

"Is it? You're missing the skyscrapers and the world-class ethnic food and the museums and Broadway."

"Maybe. But that doesn't mean I'm criticizing your home. You love it here."

"I do. But I've traveled, Abby. I know what the world has to offer."

"May I ask you a question?"

She saw him frown slightly. "Of course."

"Why did you come to Appaloosa Island today?"

His chest rose and fell as he sighed deeply. "The truth?"

"Yes, please."

"You intrigue me, Abby. My personal life has been pretty boring for the last year and a half. The pool of available romantic partners in Royal—for someone like me who has always lived here—is finite. You're new and different, and I wanted to spend time with you."

Her stomach flipped. Here was an übermasculine man, not a boy, stating unequivocally that he was interested. What was she going to do about that?

"Does this mean you're willing to let me film you at your ranch?"

He winced. "I'm still debating."

"So, what you're dangling is carte blanche as a videographer if I consent to get better acquainted with you?"

He grimaced. "This isn't a negotiation. One has nothing to do with the other."

"Well, if you let me film you, we'll be spending *lots* of time together."

"I'm not interested in being cast as some token

rancher for your viewers. I am who I am. It's nothing exotic."

"For a city dweller, this lifestyle you've chosen has a certain je ne sais quoi."

"That's what I'm talking about," he grumbled. "There's nothing romantic and exciting about sweat and dirt and cows."

"Familiarity breeds contempt. You don't see yourself as an outsider would."

He shot her a look. "I thought you were doing a documentary about Soiree on the Bay."

"I am. But I'm beginning to realize that the town of Royal and the Texas Cattleman's Club may be as much or more interesting than a music festival that hasn't even happened yet. You see, I've picked up a lot from Lila about how things work around Maverick County. I'm still after the human interest angle."

"Well, good luck with that."

Carter pulled off onto the side of the road. He reached across her lap and opened the glove box. "Here. If I'm putting the top down, you'll need this."

This was a narrow silk scarf, clearly expensive. It was deep amber scattered with tiny navy fleur-de-lis. When he leaned close, Abby inhaled his scent. Probably whatever he had shaved with that morning. Lime... And a hint of something else.

Her pulse beat faster. It was a relief when he straightened.

She pulled her hair to the nape of her neck and secured the ponytail with the scarf, knotting it tightly.

The wind would still do a number on the loose ends, but she didn't mind that.

She watched as Carter hit the button and made sure the top retracted slowly. Then he climbed back into the driver's seat and gave her a grin that caused her knees to quiver. "Ready?"

Abby nodded, her heart beating more quickly than the moment warranted. "Hit the pedal, cowboy."

The next hour took on a surreal quality. The open road. The wind in her face. The man beside her. With a sigh, Abby leaned against the headrest and closed her eyes. Clearly, there was more to Carter than she'd first thought. This busy, successful rancher who was willing to blow a whole day chasing down a woman who might or might not sleep with him had layers. Interesting layers. *Irresistible* layers.

Texas roads were straight and flat, and Carter drove with confidence. Never once did Abby have any qualms about her safety. For the first time, she understood the appeal of a fast, sexy car and an adventurous man behind the wheel.

When they arrived in Royal, she was windblown but content. She touched Carter lightly, her fingertips registering his muscular forearm and warm skin. "I'm hungry," she admitted. "So dinner sounds great. But I should change first."

He eased into a parking spot and turned to face her. His blue eyes reflected the sky. "Only if you want to. Your dress is beautiful." He paused. "And so are you." His gaze roved from her face to her breasts and back up to her eyes, making her shiver despite the heat.

Her throat tightened. Were all cowboys so direct? She licked her lips, telling herself they were dry from the hot summer breeze. "Um…thank you. But I'd feel more comfortable if I could shower and change."

"Whatever you want. It's still early. An hour and a half? I'll make a reservation at Sheen. It's a newer restaurant. I think you'll like it."

"How dressy?"

"Anything similar to what you're wearing."

At the hotel, Carter pulled up under the portico and they both got out of the car. He retrieved her belongings from the back seat. "I'll run out to the ranch and be back to pick you up around six thirty." Casually, he kissed her cheek. "See you soon, Abby."

She stood and watched as he gunned the engine and sped away around the corner.

In the elevator, she barely recognized her reflection in the mirrored glass. Her cheeks glowed with a deep rosy hue. Slowly, her smile faded.

She was getting off track. She had come to Royal to make a documentary and get her career on solid footing. Flirting with a sexy rancher wasn't on the list.

Even so, as she showered, washed her hair and changed into another dress, nothing could block Carter from her thoughts. Or erase the feel of his hot lips burning against her skin.

He was dangerous. Why would she get involved with a man, even temporarily, whose worldview was so different from hers?

She would have to tread carefully. Needing him for her documentary was one thing. Tumbling into his bed was another entirely.

Four

Going home to the ranch was a mistake. Too many people needed to ask Carter too many questions. By the time he escaped the inquisition, showered and changed, he barely had enough time to make it back into town to pick up Abby at her hotel at the appointed hour.

As he drove to get her, he thought about the day. He'd had fun. Honestly, that was never high on his list these days. Responsibility, yes. Hard work, definitely. But fun? Not really.

Abby made him want things. Lots of things. Sex, of course. She was real and beautiful, and he couldn't deny the powerful attraction. But it was more than that. She represented a time in his life when he still had choices. At her age, he'd been actively working on the ranch, but had still entertained the idea that he might ultimately do something other than be a rancher.

Unfortunately, his dad had suffered a heart attack when Carter was twenty-five, and soon after, his life was mapped out for him. He hadn't minded. He loved the ranch. But it had been a shock to go from his carefree postcollege days to being the top dog.

And then there was the whole thing with Madeline. His gut clenched. He'd been wrong about her. *So wrong.* Was Abby too much like his ex-fiancée? Did he have a type? Was he setting himself up for embarrassment and hurt again?

The unpleasant thought was one he didn't want to dwell on, especially since his libido was firmly in the driver's seat. He shoved the past into a locked box where it belonged and concentrated on the evening ahead.

Abby met him in the lobby. She had changed into another sexy outfit, this one more sophisticated, but no less flattering. The sleeveless, knee-length dress was white jersey knit. It clung to her body in ways that probably should be outlawed in the presence of red-blooded males. The bodice plunged in a deep vee, where a gold necklace dangled. Again, her shoulders were bare, her hair was loose and she wore white espadrilles with three-inch cork heels. The laces crisscrossed around her ankles.

He closed the distance between them. "You look amazing," he said. When he kissed her cheek lightly, she seemed flustered.

The restaurant wasn't far away. Over dinner, they spoke of less personal topics. Abby was funny and smart and well-informed. He should have expected that from a woman who spent time on both coasts. She might only be twenty-four, but she had grown up in a privileged atmosphere with a top-notch education.

Carter liked the fact that she challenged him. The conversation was stimulating and wide-ranging. She kept him on his toes. And underneath their back-and-forth was a slow, molten sexual awareness.

He knew it was too soon to sleep with her. He thought she wanted him, but a man needed to be sure. On the other hand, maybe he could speed things along with a little cooperation.

Over dessert, he played his best card. "I've decided I'm willing to let you do some filming at the ranch, within reason. How about coming over for lunch tomorrow?"

Abby wrinkled her nose. "I'm glad to hear that, but I already have plans. Lila has arranged for me to sit in on a meeting of the advisory board for the festival. I think we'll be at the Texas Cattleman's Club."

"Ah." Now he was really frustrated.

"I could come the next day," she said, perhaps reading his mood. Big brown eyes focused on him intently. She reached across the table and patted his hand. "I appreciate the invitation, Carter. Really, I do. But this meeting is important."

"Of course it is," he replied. "I understand."

"May I make a personal observation?" she asked quietly.

He stared at her, trying to read her thoughts. His fingers itched to tangle in her hair, to pull her closer and press his lips to hers. To hold her and trace the curves of her body beneath that soft, clingy dress. "Personal?" The word came out a little hoarse.

Abby nodded. "If you don't mind."

So polite. So incredibly enticing.

"Sure," he said. "I have no secrets."

When she swallowed, the muscles in her slender throat moved visibly. For the first time, he realized she was not as calm as he had imagined. "I get the feeling," she said, "that you want to sleep with me. Am I way off base?"

After nearly choking on his tongue, he found his voice. "Are you always so direct?" Her question rattled him.

"I don't play games, if that's what you mean. Most men and women make things too complicated."

"What happens if I say yes?"

"Well…" She stared at her hands clasped on the white linen tablecloth. "I'd probably explain that it's too soon." She looked up at him from beneath her lashes.

His breathing hitched. "So, you're saying there *is* a hypothetical date that might *not* be too soon?"

Her smile was slow and mysterious. "Precisely. I like you, Carter. A lot. But there are things to consider."

"Such as?" He would bat them all down one by one.

"I've never in my life slept with a man I've known only two days. Or two weeks for that matter."

He felt his advantage slipping. "Is there a *but* in there?"

"Not really. The problem is, you and I have nothing in common, and I'm only going to be in Royal for a limited time. I don't know if I'm willing to do short-term with you. It might be better to settle for flirting and friendship."

"Nope," he said, scowling. "Not a choice. I have friends, Abby. You don't fall into that category."

"Acquaintances then? Or business associates?"

Was she taunting him? The fact that he wasn't sure frustrated him. Or maybe it was the need pulsing in his gut. "I don't have to label anything, Abby. We'll be who we are. If that leads to sex, I'm all for it."

Abby trembled. Had she ever met a man who was so earthy and civilized at the same time? Carter wasn't rude or crass, but he took no pains to hide his sexual desire. For *her*. She was both flattered and intimidated. Could she hold her own with so much testosterone? Carter was a man who knew what he wanted and wasn't shy about going for it.

She suspected that a woman in his bed would find incredible pleasure. And she wanted him. No question. Still, sex and men had been tripping up women for millennia.

In her adult life, she had been disappointed by a few guys. She'd misjudged a couple of others. Not once had she faced heartbreak. Maybe that said something about her tolerance for risk. She always calculated the odds for success in any situation.

Carter Crane might turn out to be her weak spot. The strength of her desire for him was enough to make her put on the brakes. It would be dangerous and indulgent to embark on an affair when she was in the midst of a possibly career-changing project.

"Fair enough," she said. "No labels. No clock. No expectations."

His grin was tight. "I'm expecting plenty, gorgeous. But you'll have to make the call. Agreed?"

She nodded, her stomach fluttery. "Agreed."

"Dessert?"

"Yes, please."

Because looking at Carter was making her rethink her sensible approach, she scanned the restaurant. It was beautiful, made almost entirely of glass. An interested patron could observe a chef at work or track the sunset.

Sheen was hugely popular, not only because it was new, but because the food was spectacular. Every table was full. Over strawberry crepes slathered in real whipped cream, she eyed her dinner companion. Although earlier he had tried to convince her she didn't need to change for the evening, she was glad she had.

It was true that some diners had come in casual attire, but at least three-quarters of the men and women around them were dressed in what Abby would call special occasion clothes. The clientele ranged from the occasional high school couple on a date, to clusters of business associates, to folks like Carter and Abby enjoying a night out.

She was sad to see the evening end. Being with the ruggedly handsome rancher made her feel alive and intensely feminine in a way that was novel and exciting. Still, she was cautious. He could coax her into bed with little effort on his part. That knowledge was sobering.

If she wasn't ready for such a rash decision, she needed to limit her exposure to him.

She licked the last dab of whipped cream off her spoon and set it on her plate with an inward sigh of appreciation for the pastry chef's expertise. "I should probably get back to the hotel. I still have some prep work to do for my lunch meeting tomorrow."

Carter's face was oddly expressionless. "Of course." He dealt with the check and then escorted her between tables to the front door.

The night was perfect. A summer moon. A light breeze. Unfortunately, the trip back to the hotel was quick. Carter parked the convertible just around the corner from the main entrance beneath a dim street-light. He'd kept the top up this time.

She jumped out, bent on escaping her own wants and needs. Carter met her on the sidewalk and put a hand on her wrist. "A good-night kiss? Or is that too much to ask…"

Her legs trembled. "I'd like that," she said.

When his lips covered hers, it was like jumping off a cliff into unknown waters. Her stomach shot to her throat and dropped again, leaving her woozy and breathless.

He held her with confidence. One big male hand settled on the curve of her ass. She made a small noise, somewhere between a whimper and a moan, when he pulled her more tightly into his embrace. Her arms curled around his neck.

His body was hard everywhere hers was soft. She smelled the scent of his skin, trying to memorize it.

How had she known from almost the first moment that he was the one? Not *the* one as in gold rings and white picket fences, but the one who could reveal everything she had kept tightly furled inside her.

Carter's reckless passion burned through her inhibitions, her ironclad caution. They were on a public street just off the central thoroughfare, somewhat secluded this time of night, but in plain view of anyone who might happen by. Truthfully, he could have taken her against the hood of the car, and she might not have protested.

When she felt the urgent press of his erection against her abdomen, she knew one of them had to keep a clear head.

Though it pained her to do so, she put a hand against his chest and pushed. "Carter…"

To his credit, he released her immediately.

They faced each other in the shadowy illumination from overhead.

"Do I need to apologize?" he asked gruffly.

It was impossible to read his expression. "No. Not at all. Thank you for dinner. I enjoyed our evening. And thank you for driving me home this afternoon from the island. I'm touched that you gave up an entire day for me."

He shook his head slowly, his jawline grim. "I'm beginning to think I'd do just about anything for you. Which makes you a dangerous woman."

She traced his chin with a fingertip, feeling the late-day stubble. "I like that. No one's ever called me dangerous before."

"You don't have a clue…"

Was he feeding her a line? Spinning a tale of a man made vulnerable by sex? How could she believe that?

She knew she was attractive in a casual, understated way. The male sex responded to her. But she was no femme fatale, luring unsuspecting men into reckless behavior. That was a ludicrous notion.

Still, she wanted to trust his words, wanted to believe that he felt the same urgent pull she did. Pheromones were a powerful thing. That didn't mean she and Carter were kindred spirits. It only meant they wanted to jump each other's bones.

With reluctance, she made herself step back. "Good night, Carter."

His eyes glittered. "Good night, Abby."

Turning her back on him as she walked away felt risky, but she had to get inside.

"I'll make sure you get to the door," he said, following her at a short distance.

"It's only a few steps." She picked up the pace.

"A gentleman doesn't drop a lady on a street corner."

By the time Abby made it to the portico where the doorman stood, her heart was pounding. Carter had lingered on the sidewalk. She felt his gaze on her back as she headed for the double glass doors.

She wanted badly to turn around. But she kept on walking…

After a remarkably peaceful night, given her jumbled thoughts and feelings, Abby awoke ready to meet the day. She was determined to focus on her job and not the enigmatic Carter Crane.

Lila had offered to pick her up again, but Abby waved her off. It was time to get acquainted with the town of Royal. Besides, the Texas Cattleman's Club was only a few blocks away. Even with her camera and tote, it was easily within walking distance.

Today, she dressed in black dress pants and a cream blazer over a cinnamon silk tank. The jacket had large, quirky black buttons. When she was ready, she glanced at herself in the mirror. The only jewelry she wore was a pair of onyx studs she had purchased from an artisan in Sedona. Her black espadrilles were comfortable enough for the stroll, but nice enough to complement her outfit.

She debated what to do with her hair. Her preference was to leave it loose, but it was going to be very hot today. In the end, she twined it in a loose French braid.

When she had grabbed what she would need for the morning and then exited the hotel, she realized she was nervous. The people who would attend this meeting today were key players in Royal's high-powered business scene. It took a lot of money and influence to pull off an event like Soiree on the Bay.

Seeing the famed Texas Cattleman's Club in person was fascinating. The imposing edifice dated back to 1910, though it had been updated over the years. The large, rambling single-story building was constructed of dark stone and wood with a tall slate roof. Though once an all-male enclave, the onetime "old boys' club" now welcomed females into the membership.

Inside was even more impressive. Super high ceilings, large windows and, of course, the ubiquitous hunting trophies and historical artifacts displayed on paneled walls. Abby liked history as much as the next person, but dead animal heads weren't her thing.

The meeting was to start at ten. She had arrived at nine thirty. After gawking in the spacious foyer, she spoke with the receptionist and showed her credentials. The woman directed her to a conference room down a broad hallway.

Lila was already there, setting out water glasses and pens and paper. She looked up when Abby walked in. "Hey, Abby. I'm glad you're early. I made up a cheat sheet for you."

"A cheat sheet?" she asked.

"Yeah, I thought you could use a head start. It's confusing when they all start talking at once. Do you want me to introduce you formally?"

"Whatever you think. Honestly, I wouldn't mind being the proverbial fly on the wall. At least until I get my bearings."

"Then we'll do that," Lila said cheerily. She handed Abby a sheet of paper. "This isn't everyone, but it's the core of the group. I copied their pictures in color and gave you a brief bio of each."

"Excellent." While Lila finished her prep work, Abby took a seat at the back of the room against the wall. The main participants would be seated around the large, beautifully polished conference table.

She had studied up on the main players already. Russell Edmond—Rusty—was the oft-married patriarch of the überwealthy family. His money came from oil, and he owned a massive, luxurious ranch outside of town. It was his three children, Russell Jr., known as Ross, Gina Edmond and Asher Edmond, who were spearheading the festival.

When the door opened and the principals began arriving, she put aside her cheat sheet and concentrated on learning about the actors involved. Ross Edmond—tall and lanky with dirty blond hair and blue eyes—was impossible to miss. He had the innate confidence that comes with wealth.

His sister, Gina, had gorgeous dark hair and eyes and was super stylish. She looked to be close to Abby's age. That left the other Edmond sibling, Asher, who, according to Lila's cheat sheet, was actually a stepbrother. Odd, because his close-cropped brown hair and brown eyes resembled Gina's. Even at first glance, he seemed the most intense of the trio.

There were a few other people entering the room in a trickle, but it was soon clear they were either assistants or people like Lila who represented the town of Royal in various capacities.

That left only one unidentified player. According to Lila's info, his name was Billy Holmes. Somehow, he was involved with the Edmonds in planning the festival.

Abby had to admit he was gorgeous. Black hair, pale green eyes and scruffy facial hair gave him a roguish presence. He smiled. A lot. At *everyone*. Who was he, and how did he fit into this scenario?

Ross Edmond convened the meeting. Apparently, all the heavy lifting had been accomplished in earlier gatherings. Today was about tying up loose ends and making sure everyone was on the same page.

Abby listened carefully, making notes about anything she thought might have a bearing on her film.

At a lull in the conversation, Lila stood and motioned toward Abby. "I want you all to meet Abby Carmichael. She's the documentary filmmaker I've told you about. If the festival goes well, Abby's work will help lift our visibility to the next level and ensure that the festival continues for years to come."

Abby smiled and nodded, well aware that no one was particularly interested in what she had to offer. Except perhaps Billy Holmes. His grin seemed personal, and he looked her over carefully. The perusal fell just shy of being inappropriate. She had met men like him. If any female appeared on their radar, they *had* to make a good impression.

Eventually, the meeting wound to a close. There was a sense of urgency, given that the festival was only weeks away. After months of planning, everything was finally falling into place.

As Lila did her job, chatting with everyone and gathering up the materials she had brought with her, Abby was disconcerted to realize that Billy Holmes had lingered and was making a beeline in her direction.

She stood and smiled politely. "Hello, Mr. Holmes. I wonder if I might interview you in a few days. I'm sure you're a very busy man."

He reached out to shake her hand. "I always have time for anyone who wants to promote the festival."

Abby hesitated. "Well, I'm not *promoting* the festival

per se. I'm a visual storyteller. Soiree on the Bay—along with the town of Royal—promises to be an interesting project. But of course, my film won't be out anytime soon."

"Doesn't matter. We want the festival to be such a big hit it will go on for years."

"You sound like a man with a vision."

"I like to think so." He glanced at his watch. "I've gotta run. How about Thursday at eleven for your interview? Would you like to see the Elegance Ranch? I live in a guesthouse on the Edmonds' property. I'll get my housekeeper to feed us."

"Sure," Abby said, wondering if she might be getting in over her head. Billy Holmes seemed nice enough, but she couldn't figure out where he fit in with the Edmond clan and the festival. Until she did, she would be on her guard.

As Billy walked out of the room, Lila joined Abby. "Well, what did you think?"

"I think people with a lot of money are a different breed."

Lila cocked her head, smiling gently. "Your father owns a Malibu beach house and your mom is a Manhattan socialite. You're hardly scraping by."

Abby grimaced. "Fair point. But you know what I mean. The Edmond family has buckets of cash. Not to mention land and influence. Here in Texas, they're practically royalty. Now that I've met several of them, I'm seeing a new direction for my film. Maybe the documentary will be less about the festival and more about the people who can pull off such a feat. What do you think?"

Lila held up her hands. "Not my area of expertise. But the Edmonds *are* fascinating, that's for sure. What's next on your schedule?"

"I've asked Carter Crane to let me do some filming on his ranch. You know, for local color."

The other woman grinned. "How was the drive yesterday? You must have made a big impression on the man."

Abby felt her face get hot. "It was a fun afternoon. I like him. And I think the camera will *love* him…those sharp cut features and strong chin."

"I'm surprised he's agreed to that. Carter likes to keep a low profile."

"I'm not sure how much latitude he'll give me. But I'm hopeful."

Lila sobered without warning, her expression serious. "Be careful, Abby. I wouldn't want you to get hurt."

Five

Abby's stomach curled with anxiety. "What's wrong with Carter? He's been a perfect gentleman as far as I can tell."

"I feel bad gossiping, but you need to know the truth. Carter keeps women at a distance, particularly women like you."

"Women like *me*? What in the heck does that mean?" She was mildly insulted. And worried.

Lila perched on the edge of the table, one leg swinging. "Carter was engaged to a woman from Chicago a few years ago. Madeline moved to Royal, and they began planning a wedding. But the next thing I knew, the festivities were canceled and the two of them were officially over. Apparently, Madeline hated life 'in the sticks' as she called it. She missed her big-city life, and she detested cows and horses and dust."

"Oh." Abby felt stupid and small. Maybe Carter was just playing with her. "Thank you for telling me," she muttered.

"I hope I haven't stepped over the line," Lila said, her expression conveying both worry and concern. "But if I weren't a happily engaged woman, Carter Crane might give *me* a few heart palpitations. He's macho and sexy and aloof. The trifecta when it comes to attracting the female sex."

"He *is* handsome."

"Maybe I shouldn't have said anything," Lila fretted.

Abby summoned a light tone. "I barely know the man. But I appreciate the information." She picked up her bag. "I'd better head out. Plenty to do. Thanks for letting me sit in on this meeting. It helped a lot."

"Sure," Lila said. "And let me know if there's anything else you need."

As Abby walked down Main Street, she tried to absorb the feel of the place. It's true that the town wasn't huge. Maverick County was mostly rural. But still, there was an upscale feel to the buildings and the businesses. Perhaps because oil money and cattle money had a far reach. Good schools. Great roads. This was no backwoods holler.

Her stomach growled, reminding her that lunch was next on the agenda. On a whim, she popped into the Royal Diner. Its 1950s retro decor and red, white and black color scheme were charming. When Abby had asked her hotel concierge for recommendations, he told her the diner was top-notch, and that the owner, Amanda Battle, was the sheriff's wife.

Now Abby slid into a red faux leather booth and tucked her things on the seat beside her. The menu offerings made her mouth water. When the pleasant older waitress stopped by the table, Abby ordered a vanilla milkshake, a tuna melt with fries and a glass of water. It had been a long time since she had indulged in such comfort food. Her mother was always dieting, and her father was a vegan.

When the meal arrived, Abby dug in with enthusiasm. Often while eating alone, she used the time to "people watch" or to get ideas down on paper. Today, she did both. With a sandwich in one hand and a pen in the other, she began filling a small notebook with her observations from today's meeting.

The Edmond siblings each had distinct personalities. She didn't know what to make of Billy Holmes. Perhaps her interview with him would uncover interesting layers. Often, people were more at ease in their home settings, so she wasn't averse to meeting him out at the ranch. He might even give her access to the Edmond family members if she decided to explore that route.

She had finished her sandwich and was nibbling on the last of her fries when she realized two women had taken the booth right behind hers—the one that had been vacant when she arrived. Abby tried not to eavesdrop, but the hushed conversation turned interesting quickly.

Though the women were conversing in lowered voices, Abby was only inches away. The words *festi-*

val and *money* caught her attention immediately. Unfortunately, she couldn't hear every single phrase. But the gist of the topic was clear: the women seemed to be discussing the possibility that someone had taken a large sum of money from the festival coffers.

Abby's eyes widened. Not a hint about finances had come up during the advisory board meeting, nor a whiff of a problem. Were the members of the board hiding something, or was she overhearing idle gossip?

Unfortunately, the waitress brought Abby's check. There were customers waiting to be seated, so it seemed rude to linger. As she stood and picked up her belongings, she glanced at the women in the booth behind her. Neither of them was remarkable.

But what she heard stuck with her.

She spent the next couple of hours exploring Royal, filming anything that caught her fancy. Historic buildings. Quirky shop signs. Kids playing in a park. Though the town definitely possessed an almost palpable energy, that feeling was balanced by a sense that life was comfortable here. Predictable. *Enjoyable.*

Despite the fact that she was definitely out of her element, she had to acknowledge that Royal was interesting and charming. People were friendly. More than once, she found herself embroiled in a sidewalk conversation. In a community where everybody knew everybody, Abby apparently stood out.

She didn't mind the attention, not really. But after a few hours of walking the streets, she was more than ready to head back to the hotel. Getting clean, donning comfy pajamas and watching TV sounded like the perfect way to unwind.

The only irritant marring her peaceful afternoon was knowing that Carter hadn't called or texted. When he invited her to his ranch, she'd had to wave him off because of the advisory board meeting. Unfortunately, he hadn't said a word about tomorrow or the next day or the day after that.

When she got back to her room, she decided to be proactive…

Hi, Carter. Is it okay if I come out to the ranch in the morning? Seven-ish? I'd love to do some filming with the morning light. If there are no gates to unlock, I won't even have to bother you.

After a moment's hesitation, she hit Send. Then she turned her phone facedown and headed for the shower.

Carter rolled over in bed and glanced at the clock— 5:00 a.m. He had no reason to be up at this hour, but he'd been dreaming. Hot, sensual, disturbing dreams.

And all because Abby Carmichael was coming out to his ranch. He slung an arm over his head and stretched, feeling the brush of cool sheets against his hot skin.

Already he knew the shape of her body, the sound of her voice, the scent of her skin. At this particular moment, he felt like a hormonal teenager about to catch a glimpse of his high school crush.

The difference was, he and Abby were consenting adults, fully capable of making rash decisions.

By the time he showered and dressed and gobbled down some breakfast, he was jittery as hell. He didn't want to be interviewed, and he didn't want to be filmed. But he *did* want more time with Abby, so he was stuck.

In their text exchange last night, she had offered to stay away from the house. Abby claimed to want ethereal shots of the stables and the pastures and the corrals bathed in warm light. She promised not to get in the way of any ranch operations.

Did she really think he would ignore her presence? Surely, she wasn't that naive or clueless. That one kiss they shared had been incendiary and left him wanting more.

He walked out back to the barn and saddled up his horse. As a teenager, he had sometimes slept until noon. Now he had come to appreciate the mystical purity of the early morning. A man could think and plan and contemplate taking risks at this time of day. The slight chill in the air was invigorating—even more so because it was fleeting.

Carter galloped along the gravel and dirt road that bisected the ranch, squinting into the strengthening rays of the sun. It was after eight now. Where was she?

And then he spotted her. She had parked her rental car at the edge of the road and was climbing the fence to get a shot of sunflowers. Carter hadn't planted them. They were his mother's legacy. But he had to admit, they made his heart swell with happiness and pride every time he passed them.

Sunset Acres had been passed into his keeping. Carter had a duty to perform. And he was working his ass off to make sure the ranch remained healthy and viable.

As he approached his visitor, he slowed the horse to a trot. Abby seemed to not notice his presence yet. She was intent on her task. With the camera balanced on her shoulder and one leg wrapped around the fence, she was perched precariously.

He didn't want to startle her.

Instead, he tied off the horse and covered the last few yards on foot.

"Abby," he said quietly. "Good morning."

After a split second, she half turned and looked over her free shoulder at him. "Carter. I didn't hear you."

"I could tell." Then he noticed her earbuds. "Ah. You're listening to music."

She shook her head, grimacing. "No." She lowered the camera. "It's a podcast."

"About?"

She shrugged. "Learning to take chances. Building self-confidence. Stuff like that."

"All set?" he asked.

"Yes."

"Then let me help you down. Camera first."

She handed it over without argument and watched him as he placed it carefully on the seat of her car. Then he lifted his arms. "Come off that fence, Ms. Photographer. Before you break your neck."

When he settled his hands on her waist, she leaned forward and let him take her weight. She was thin. Maybe too thin. But she was really tall for a woman, so perhaps that accounted for it. In the split second when he held her completely with her slender body pressed to his, his heart punched hard.

Carefully, he let her slide to her feet. She stumbled, but he steadied her.

"Thanks, Carter," she murmured.

There it was again. That odd and disarming way she pronounced his name.

"I thought you might stop by the house to say hello," he muttered, swamped by a wave of need so intense it made him tremble.

Abby swept her hands through her hair. "I didn't want to wake you. Or catch you in the shower."

"Perhaps you could have joined me."

Her eyes opened wide. A tinge of pink darkened her cheeks. "Still too soon," she muttered. But her body language was not as negative as her words. She had plenty of room to step away, to put distance between them. Yet she was so close he could feel the brush of her breath against his ear.

He had to get a grip. Clearing his throat, he focused his gaze just past her shoulder, telling himself he was imagining the strength of his arousal. It was deprivation. That's all. He needed a woman. *Any* woman. Abby Carmichael was nothing special.

"Did you get the early morning shots you wanted?" The words came out husky and slow as if he were seducing her, not asking a mundane question.

Abby nodded. "Most of them. With your permission, I'd like to come back at sunset to shoot some more."

"You could stay all day," he said, brushing his thumb

across her cheekbone. "You know, shadow me. See how things work."

Her smile was rueful. "You're a man used to getting what he wants."

"Not always. But yes, frequently."

"I suppose it doesn't help my case if I admit that I want what you want."

He sucked in a sharp breath. "Not fair, Abby. Not when you're asking to take things slowly."

She toyed with a button on his shirt, one right near his heart. "I didn't expect a complication like you when I came to Royal. You're perfect for my documentary. Beyond that, I'm not so sure."

He lifted her chin with his fingertip and brushed a light kiss over her soft lips. "Why don't we let things unfold and see what happens?"

At last, she backed away. Big brown eyes stared at him. "I suppose I could do that."

"Do you ride? Horses," he clarified, since she seemed dazed.

"No."

"I could put you up on Foxtrot with me. Show you the ranch. You won't have to do a thing but hold on."

"Foxtrot?" Abby raised an eyebrow.

"He's been known to do some fancy footwork when he doesn't want to be ridden."

"Sounds dangerous."

"I won't let you fall," he reassured her.

"What about my car?"

"Leave it here. No one will bother it."

"Do you think I could film on horseback?" she wondered aloud.

"I have no idea, but you're welcome to try." He watched as she glanced from him to his horse and back again.

"Okay," she said. "It might be fun."

He ignored the jolt of jubilation that fizzed in his veins. Abby was wearing a thin, orangey-red cotton shirt over a white camisole and a pair of pale denim skinny jeans with artful holes at the knees. Her sneakers were white Keds, already stained by the Texas soil. It wasn't exactly riding attire, but he supposed it would have to do...

He held out a hand. "Shall we?"

Abby was no dummy. She knew what kind of trouble she was courting. But she couldn't stop herself. Ignoring Carter's outstretched arm, she sidled around him and headed for her car. Fortunately, the enormous horse was tethered in the opposite direction.

In the end, she decided it would be too awkward to hold her video camera and cling to Carter at the same time. For the record, she knew there would be plenty of clinging. By the time she put her camera away, locked the car and pocketed her keys, Carter had already mounted the beautiful glossy black stallion.

As she walked back to meet him, he stared at her. The intensity of his gaze was as intimate as a caress. Beneath her top, her nipples beaded. The day was heating up, but she couldn't blame her rapid heartbeat on the rising temperatures.

When she was six feet away, Carter leaned down and held out his hand, smiling as if this was no big deal. "Put your left foot on the heel of my boot to steady yourself," he said. "I'll pull you up, and you swing your right leg over."

"You make it sound so easy." She hesitated, trying to remember every movie she had ever seen where the heroine joined the hero on horseback. There weren't that many. Especially not ones filmed in the twenty-first century. "I don't want to be responsible for pulling your arm out of its socket or tearing your rotator cuff."

"You're stalling, Abby. Don't overthink it."

"Couldn't I climb on top of the fence and do it from there?"

"Where's the romance in that?" His broad grin taunted her.

Still, she paused. In the course of her dating life, she had been acquainted with a few very wealthy men. But they were generally ensconced behind corporate desks and wore suits. She had also known surfers and ballplayers and gym rats who prided themselves on their hard bodies and athletic prowess.

Carter was a disturbing mix of both wealthy confidence and masculine strength. He didn't posture or preen. He was who he was. The whole package.

Stifling her doubts, she reached out and took his hand. His grip was firm and sure. As soon as he saw that she had situated her foot as he had instructed, he tugged her up behind him. The entire maneuver took mere seconds. She landed in the saddle with a startled exhalation.

And then she looked at the ground. Her arms clenched around his waist as her knees quivered. She hadn't realized how high off terra firma she would be.

With her cheek pressed against Carter's back and her fingers in a death grip on the front of his belt, she tried to calm down.

"You okay back there?" he asked.

She wanted to hate the amused chuckle in his voice, but she was too busy relying on him to keep her from a painful death. "Just peachy," she bit out, rounding up all the sarcasm she could find and stuffing it into those two words.

Carter set the horse in motion and laughed harder. "Is it a fear of heights that's getting you, or the horse?"

The breeze whipped her hair in her face. "The horse is fine. And it's not a fear of heights. It's a fear of hitting the ground in a bloody, broken mess."

Carter laid his free hand over both of hers, stroking her knuckles in a move that shouldn't have been particularly erotic, but did in fact send arousal pulsing from her scalp to her toes.

"You're safe, Abby. I swear. Now, how do you feel about speed?"

Six

Carter was enjoying himself immensely. Abby was plastered against his back as if he could protect her from every source of harm. He didn't want her to be scared, but he liked having her close.

He gave Foxtrot free rein as Carter took Abby from one end of the ranch to the other, looking at it through her eyes, pointing out every spot that had meaning for him. From the small corral where he learned to ride as a five-year-old to the copse of cottonwood trees where he had his first kiss a decade later, this ranch was home.

Occasionally, they stopped, and he lifted Abby down, taking advantage of the situation to flirt with her while he showed her a new barn or an old steer—the saddle shop or the historic bunkhouse. Abby was enthusiastic, but always in the context of her documentary.

Never once did he get the impression that she saw things through *his* eyes.

A Texas ranch was a novelty to her, perhaps even beautiful in a certain context. But Abby was a city girl. It was a truth he'd do well to remember.

Eventually, they both gave in to hunger—for food. He dropped her off at her car, and then rode ahead to show her the way to his house.

When they went inside, Abby's genuine praise soothed some of his disgruntlement.

"This is gorgeous, Carter! I love it."

As she wandered from room to room, he followed her, remembering the choices he had made with a designer. Comfort had always been his first priority. And natural light. Lots of windows. Furniture made for sitting.

Abby skittered past the door to his bedroom with comical haste and went on down the hall to explore the laundry room, the workout room and the small inground pool outside, just past the breezeway. When they doubled back to the living room, she smiled at him. "This is the perfect house for you. I see your stamp on every bit of it."

"When my parents moved, and I took over, they gave me their blessing to remodel extensively. At the same time, we all went in together to design a large guesthouse about a half mile from here. We're a close-knit family, but they didn't want to cramp my style when they came to visit."

She sobered. "Lila told me about your fiancée…or ex-fiancée, I should say. I'm sorry. I wasn't prying."

His jaw tightened. "You're saying she volunteered the information? And why would she do that?"

Abby chewed her bottom lip, visibly uncomfortable. "She warned me that you were not in the market for a relationship. That you'd been burned."

He slammed his fist against one of the chiseled wooden support beams. "This whole damn town needs to mind its own business."

"But they won't. Not according to you."

He exhaled, not really sure why he was so pissed. "No," he said curtly. "They won't." He turned toward the kitchen. "How do you feel about turkey and mayo sandwiches with bacon? My housekeeper comes in three time a week and keeps my fridge stocked."

"Lucky you." Abby seemed as glad as he was to move on to other topics. "And yeah, a sandwich sounds good," she said.

They ate their lunch in the small breakfast nook, enjoying the view from the large bay window. Carter was extremely aware of the woman at his side. Her scent. The sound of her voice. The enthusiastic way she devoured her meal.

She seemed to be a woman unafraid of indulging her appetites.

He shifted on his seat, realizing that he needed to focus his attention on something other than Abby's slender, toned arm, her hand almost touching his. "So, have you nailed down a theme for your documentary, an angle? You were hoping yesterday's meeting of the advisory board would help."

Abby stood and carried her plate to the sink. Then

she refilled her lemonade and returned. "It was just business, unfortunately. I did get to meet the Edmond family and see them in action."

"And?" he prodded.

"They were nice. I like them. Tell me what you know about this Billy Holmes guy. I can't figure out how he fits into all of this."

"I've only met him a handful of times," Carter told her. "He moved to Royal a few years ago. Has plenty of money. People seem to like him."

"And he lives on the Edmond estate?"

"That's what I've heard," he replied.

"I wonder why?"

Carter shrugged. "No idea. You'd have to ask him."

"I will. He and I have an interview set up for tomorrow."

Carter tensed. He had nothing concrete against Holmes, but the other man struck Carter as a womanizer. "Are you going alone?"

"Yes. Is there a problem?"

"No. But women are vulnerable. Sometimes when you don't know a person, it's better to meet on neutral ground."

"I'm having lunch at *your* house at this very moment," Abby pointed out with a mischievous grin.

"Touché."

"It will be fine. I've taken self-defense classes since I was sixteen. I can handle myself."

Carter didn't argue, but he remained mildly concerned. Maybe he could wrangle an invitation to go along as Abby's sidekick. Even as the thought formed in his head, he dismissed it. Abby would never admit she needed a bodyguard.

He let the subject drop. "So, what now? My sister always leaves a few swimsuits here. She's close to your size. Do you fancy a dip in the pool?"

"It sounds lovely, but I really want to start interviewing you on camera."

"That again?" He groaned. "I was hoping you'd moved on from that idea. Ranchers are a dime a dozen around here. The job is nothing special."

"Maybe so. But you don't see the big picture, pardon the pun. What you do here at Sunset Acres echoes the frontier cowboys of the olden days. There's poetry in it. And tradition. This probably won't be the central focus of my film, but it could serve as a powerful backdrop. Please, Carter. It won't be so bad. I promise."

He had boxed himself into a corner. By inviting her to stay the entire day, he'd all but guaranteed that she would not give up. "Fine," he grumbled. "Let's get it over with, so we can move on to something that's actually fun. Where do we do this?"

"The great room, I think."

Instead of having a traditional living room or den, Carter had designed a large, open space that could be configured in a number of ways. Despite the ample square footage, he liked to think the cozy furniture and the artwork and large windows worked together to create a welcoming atmosphere.

Abby went out to her car and returned five minutes later with the camera, a tripod and a large tote bag. "It won't take me long to set up," she assured him, practically bouncing on her feet with enthusiasm.

"I could have helped carry something," he said. "I didn't know you had so much gear."

"Well," she replied, dumping everything on the sofa, "often it's just me and the video camera, but when I'm doing serious work, I want to have all my options available." She put her hands on her hips and surveyed the room. "I think that big leather chair will be good. Can we build a fire in the fireplace?"

His brows shot to his hairline, his reaction incredulous. "It's June. In Texas."

Abby faced him, smiling sweetly. "Please, Carter. It will make the scene perfect. We can run up the AC... all right?"

His muttered response was not entirely polite. "Sure. No problem."

As he pulled together a pile of kindling, small logs and fire starter, he was conscious of Abby flitting around the room. Once she had the camera attached to the tripod, she began unfolding filters and screens to get the light exactly as she wanted it.

It was obvious she was a pro at what she did. There was no fumbling, no second-guessing. She worked with purpose, her slender hands moving at lightning speed as she manipulated settings and angles and equipment.

At last, she was satisfied. "Will you take a seat in the chair, so I can take a look?"

He sat down, feeling stiff and ridiculous. "I don't want to be turned into some romanticized stereotype. That's insulting."

"Quit being grumpy. I would never do that to you."

She touched his leg, rearranged his arm, smoothed the collar of his blue button-down shirt. With every moment that passed, he grew more and more uneasy. And more horny.

At last, Abby was satisfied.

Almost.

She peered through the camera and wrinkled her nose. "Would you mind grabbing your Stetson? We can place it artfully on the arm of the chair or on the back near your shoulder."

He glowered, ready to end this before it started. "I don't wear a hat inside the house."

"I'm not asking you to wear it. I just want it for the ambience."

"No," he said firmly. "*This*—" he waved a hand at the ridiculous fire "—is plenty."

"Fine." Abby sulked, but it was a cute sulk.

His fingers dug into the supple leather of the chair arm. "Can we please get started? This fire is making me sweat…"

Abby could tell she was losing her reluctant subject. Carter was visibly fidgety. Was it weird that his irritability made him more attractive to her? She must be seriously messed up. Or maybe she was tired of slick guys who thought they could fast-talk a woman out of her clothes. Carter was rougher around the edges. More real.

She took a sip from her water bottle and ignored her jumpy pulse. "I'm going to ask you a series of questions.

Talk as long as you want on each topic. None of this will be included word for word, but during the editing process, I'll pull out bits that complement the documentary as a whole. Does that make sense?"

"Sure."

She checked the camera once again to make sure Carter was still framed nicely, and then hit the record button. "Tell me more about how you came to run the ranch," she began, giving him an encouraging smile. She had learned that many people were not comfortable on camera, but if she got them talking, they loosened up. "You're a wealthy man. Couldn't you simply hire a manager?"

Carter grinned. "I'm pretty hands-on."

"And why is that?"

"I suppose it's what I learned growing up. My sister and I ran wild. Very few rules except for being home in time for dinner. My father worked long hours. He and my mother had a very traditional marriage. He'd come home tired and dirty at six, sometimes later."

"And why didn't *he* hire a manager?"

"It goes back a couple of generations. My dad's grandfather died in a riding accident when Dad was only seven years old. So my grandfather groomed *my* father from a very early age. Dad was used to working sunup to sundown. Those were the years when the ranch really boomed. The money was pouring in, and my father loved what he did. When my grandfather passed on, he left the entire ranch to my dad."

"That's a lot of responsibility," she remarked.

"Definitely. But my dad never questioned his role.

Unfortunately, my grandfather wasn't a fan of organized education. Dad never had the opportunity to go to college. But Sunset Acres was his consolation prize."

"Some prize."

"Yes," he acknowledged. "My mom is from Royal, too. They were schoolmates. She fit right in with the ranching lifestyle, because she'd had a similar upbringing. After they got married, they spent the next two decades and more building the ranch into an even bigger operation."

"But you mentioned health issues?"

"He had a massive heart attack when I was a year older than you are. We almost lost him." A shadow crossed Carter's face. "The doctor said it was imperative that Dad cut back on both the physical labor and the stress, but my mother knew Dad too well. She realized he couldn't *play* at being a rancher. So she convinced him to retire and hand over the reins and the keys and the headaches to me. They moved to Florida and threw themselves into fishing and boating and everything else that comes with a carefree lifestyle."

"How did you cope in the beginning?" she asked.

"It was scary as hell, I'll admit it. I had a good roster of men working under me, but knowing that the decisions were all mine was terrifying."

"Did you resent having to shoulder so much responsibility?"

His jaw tightened, his gaze stormy. "Is this a documentary or a therapy session?"

"It was just a question, Carter. You don't have to answer."

"Yes," he said, the single word flat. "I did have some negative feelings at first. I was a young male adult, intent on pursuing my own agenda. I'd finished a degree in business management, but I wasn't particularly interested in settling down."

"I'm sorry. That must have been hard."

He shrugged. "I've made my father proud. That was reason enough to put aside my personal goals. And as the years have passed, I haven't regretted that decision. This ranch is thriving. It provides jobs."

"And the legacy is unbroken," she murmured softly.

"That, too."

"I assume you'll want to pass Sunset Acres on to your own children someday?"

"Next question."

Okay. Touchy issue. She checked the viewfinder again and shifted the tripod to get a new angle. "So tell me about Madeline, your ex-fiancée."

Carter rose to his feet, glowering. "Turn off the camera." The words were curt. "I don't see how that question pertains to your documentary. If you want to ask me for personal info, Abby, please have the guts to admit that you're interested."

His sharp criticism stung, particularly because it was on point.

Flushing uncomfortably, she shut off the recording. "Sorry," she muttered. "Lila told me the bare bones. I guess I wondered how your girlfriend fit into your legacy."

"She didn't. That's why we broke up."

"How did you meet?"

He prowled, his hands shoved into his pockets. "I was in Chicago with my whole family to attend the wedding of one of my cousins. Madeline was a guest. We hit it off. There was sexual chemistry. I think both of us were looking for something and had convinced ourselves we found it."

"That must have sucked when you realized otherwise."

"Yeah, it did," he admitted gruffly. "Partly because I disappointed my mom. She was over the moon that her boy was finally settling down."

"You were running a huge ranch. That seems pretty settled to me."

"It's different. I told you…she wants grandchildren."

"Ah, yes," Abby murmured.

"Are we done with this now?" He scowled at her.

"Sure. I'd like to ask you some more questions," she said. "Not personal. More about what your days are like. The actual running of a ranching operation."

He glanced at his watch. "I have a few things I need to take care of. Why don't you make yourself at home, and I'll be back in an hour or so…"

"Do you have internet?" she asked.

"Of course I do. What kind of question is that?"

"A valid one. We're in the middle of nowhere."

His expression cooled. "Only in your eyes."

When Carter strode out of the room, Abby realized that she had let her prejudices show. No matter how rural the landscape, Royal and the surrounding environs were home to an upscale roster of citizens.

Money flowed like water apparently. These people were worldly and powerful.

She'd heard somewhere that Maverick County had more cows than people. That might not be true, but it was certainly possible. Still, the people themselves were the furthest thing from unsophisticated.

Even in the short time she had been in town, she had been forced to confront her expectations. It was becoming clear that her documentary would include entrepreneurs and politicians, society mavens and trendsetters. Blue bloods and old money. Not to mention the occasional upstart.

How was she going to capture all that and still frame Soiree on the Bay in an interesting way? The footage with Carter was a start, but she needed more.

With him gone for an hour, she was free to explore his house on her own, this time more carefully. She didn't open drawers or closets. *Duh.* She wasn't a weirdo. Instead, she walked room to room, soaking up the ambience.

She stopped at the threshold to Carter's bedroom. Even alone, she wouldn't trespass. It didn't take a psychologist to tell her that she was fascinated with his personal space. The man was intensely masculine, but he lived alone. What did he do with all that pent-up sexual energy? A little flutter low in her belly told her she wanted to find out.

It took considerable effort, but she made herself go back to the great room and deal with email. Her mother wanted to know how things were going, as did her dad. She gave them each a slightly different version of her time in Royal. After that, she watched the raw footage of Carter that she had just shot.

Holy heck, he looked good on camera. Broad shoulders, brooding good looks. And his occasional smiles were pure gold. Plus, when he talked, there was an authenticity about him, a sense of integrity. In the old days, people would have called him a straight shooter.

She ran out of things to do about the time she heard the back door slam. Carter appeared in the doorway, looking hot and windblown. "Any chance you'd be interested in that swim now?"

"Sure. As long as one of the suits fits. I'm not skinny-dipping with you, ranch man. At least not in broad daylight," she said, giving him a taunting grin.

The heat in his laser-blue gaze seared her. "Then I suppose I'll have to keep you here until dark. I grill a mean steak."

She swallowed, feeling out of her depth. She'd been teasing about the skinny-dipping, but Carter appeared to take her words at face value. "I don't want to drive back to Royal in the dark," she said, entirely serious. "I don't know these roads. I might hit an armadillo."

His face lit up with humor. "I'll take you home. One of my guys can return your car in the morning."

Well, she had run out of excuses. What did she really want? And was she brave enough to take the risk?

Seven

Carter wondered if Abby knew how expressive her face was. He swore he could read every emotion. She was flattered. And probably interested. But she was cautious, too. He could hardly blame her.

"I won't pressure you, Abby. All you have to do is say the word, and we can part as friends."

"Is there another category than friends?" Her smile was a little on the shaky side.

"You know there is. I want you. But only if you feel the same way. And beyond that, there's no timetable... Is there?"

She lifted one slender shoulder and let it fall. "Actually, yes. I won't be here more than a few weeks. That's not much time to decide whether I can trust you."

He cocked his head. "Trust me how? I'm no threat to

you, Abs." He held up his hands, palms out. "There's no quid pro quo. I'll let you interview me some more even if you and I never knock boots. You have my word."

"*Knock boots?* Are you kidding me? Is that a Texas expression? Besides, it's easy for you to be magnanimous. You know how sexy you are. I'm not sure I can keep this professional. I'm not even sure I want to…"

"So, where does that leave us?" It wouldn't do for her to know how tightly wound he was as he awaited her answer.

She grimaced. "Let's swim," she said. "After that, I don't know…"

Fifteen minutes later, when Abby exited the house and joined him in the pool, he was damn glad the water concealed his instant boner. She was the most beautiful thing he had ever seen.

And he was wrong about her being skinny. Now that she was wearing a remarkably modest, but nevertheless provocative, black two-piece swimsuit, it was painfully clear that Abby had all the curves a man could want. Long, toned legs to wrap around his waist. A flat stomach with a diamond belly button piercing that caught the sun, and breasts that were just the right size to fill a man's hands.

His fists clenched at his sides. "I see the suit fit you."

"Quit staring," she said sharply.

With no apparent self-consciousness, she walked to the end of the diving board, bounced once and made a clean dive into the pool. When she surfaced, she lifted her face to the sun and slicked back her hair, laughing.

"The water is perfect," she said. "Do you swim every day?"

"Not always." And why was that? There was no good reason other than the fact that his waking hours were busy.

Abby began doing laps, her long legs and strong arms propelling her through the water easily. Carter followed suit, careful to keep to his side of the pool. They were completely alone. None of his staff would dare seek him out without an okay ahead of time. And since he had his phone on silent, this little bubble of intimacy was intact.

At last, Abby tired. She stayed in the deep end, treading water. Finally, she clung to the metal ladder, one arm curled around the bottom step. "This is nice."

An invisible cord drew him across the pool to where she lazily kicked her legs. He stopped a few feet away, his heart pounding. Water clung to her beautiful skin in droplets that refracted the sunlight. Her eyelashes were spiky. Brown eyes stared at him as if assessing his intent.

"I'm gonna kiss you, Abs," he said hoarsely. "Unless you object."

Her eyes widened. But she didn't speak. She didn't move.

He was tall enough to touch bottom. Moving closer still, he brushed her arm. "Hang on, Abby."

Without hesitation, she released the ladder and curled her arms around his neck. Now their bodies were pressed together so closely he could feel the rapid rise and fall of her chest. All the blood left his head, rushing south.

Maybe he had heat stroke. His brain felt muzzy, and his hands tingled. "Abby…" With one arm around her back and the other hand gripping the ladder, he stared into her eyes. Deep in the midst of those chocolate irises he found tiny flecks of gold.

"Car…ter…" She caressed his name, infusing it with sensuality. Her lips curled in a smile. "This feels naughty."

"Hell, yeah…" He tried to laugh, but he didn't have enough oxygen.

She nipped his bottom lip with a tiny, stinging bite, then soothed the pain with her tongue. "You taste like chlorine," she whispered.

He yanked her closer and slammed his mouth down on hers. No smooth moves, no practiced technique. Only sheer desperation.

She met him kiss for kiss, not submitting, but battling. He wondered in some far distant corner of his brain if the heat they were conjuring would turn the pool water to steam.

If two people could devour each other, this was how it would happen. She was strong and feminine, her skin and muscles soft and smooth everywhere he was hard. Lust roared through his veins. He wanted her. But his conscience said, *too soon…*

After what seemed like an eternity, he made himself pull back. Abby's lips were swollen and puffy from his kisses. Strands of her wet hair that had dried in the sun danced around her face.

He stared at her. "We should probably find some shade," he said. "How about a lounge chair with an umbrella and a cold drink?"

Abby's expression was dazed. "Sure. Water is fine for me. But you go up the ladder first. I don't want you staring at my ass."

"Too late."

That finally made her smile.

He did as she asked, lifting himself out of the pool and deliberately shaking water at her. When Abby screeched, he chuckled. The small fridge in the pool house held chilled water bottles. He grabbed a couple of those along with some dry towels that he spread on the two chaises. Abby hovered nearby, her arms wrapped around her waist. Long, beautiful hair cascaded down her back.

"Ladies first," he said.

Abby widened the gap between the two chairs by about a foot, and then settled onto the lounger gracefully, raising her arms over her head and bending one knee.

Carter took the remaining seat and lay back with a sigh. Despite his arousal, the sensation of hot sun on his wet skin was a familiar, soothing taste of summer. Behind his sunglasses, he managed to sneak a sideways glance.

Was she asleep? Awake? He couldn't decide but chose to assume the latter. "You want to tell me more about yesterday's advisory board meeting?"

She turned her face in his direction, a half smile lifting the corners of her mouth. "Business talk?"

"It's either that or carry you to my bedroom. Seemed premature."

He witnessed her startled breath, a gasp really, quickly disguised. "I think I covered everything."

"Then let's talk about *you*."

She slung an arm over her eyes, shutting him out. But he wasn't so easily dissuaded. "Seriously, Abs, you've grilled me nonstop. And if that weren't enough, Lila blabbed about my personal life. I think it's only fair that I get to delve into your psyche."

Moving her arm, she scowled at him. "Couldn't we just have sex?"

He laughed. "You don't like being interviewed any more than I do."

"Why do you think I chose to be on this side of the camera?"

"You're only twenty-four," Carter reminded her. "How bad could your secrets be?"

"Who said I have secrets?"

He exhaled, emptying his lungs so he could inhale the scent of her again. "Everybody has secrets, Abby. But you can start with your childhood. What were you like in school?"

Her profile made him ache. Vulnerability etched her features. "I was lonely mostly. That whole mean girl stereotype is based on reality. I was a biracial kid in a sea of white faces. I was an oddity. So that put me on the outside looking in. I didn't understand why until I was seven or eight. But the first day someone said a nasty thing about my father, I was done trying to fit in. My mother went to see the principal over and over, begging for adult intervention. That only made things worse."

His stomach twisted. "I'm sorry, Abby."

"It got better in high school. There was a more diverse population. Supersmart kids whose parents had immigrated to New York as children, grown up there. I gradually built a circle of intimates, classmates with whom I could be myself." She released a breath. "In fact, my very best friend is a Pakistani woman who's now a doctor at Lenox Hill Hospital in New York. She's doing a residency in geriatric medicine. We've brainstormed about me maybe doing a documentary about the social and emotional costs of increased life span."

"Wow." Carter stared at her, for the first time understanding how complex she was, how passionate and talented. "I'm impressed, Abby. You've made an amazing life for yourself."

"It suits me. I love to travel, and I don't mind traveling alone. My parents have always given me a lot of freedom. I tried never to abuse their trust."

Silence fell between them, but it wasn't awkward. They were sizing each other up, wondering about the differences in their lives and whether there was even the tiniest bit of overlap.

He honestly didn't know. A decade separated them, though that age gap was hardly a novelty. Abby was city mouse; he was country mouse. She was happiest crisscrossing the country, whereas he had deep roots in this Texas soil.

"Do you still want to film me talking about the ranch?" he asked gruffly.

Her eyes flew open, and she turned on her side. "You don't mind?"

He tried not to notice the way her breasts nearly spilled out of her swimsuit top in that position. "It wouldn't be my first choice, but if it will help you with your project, I'll do it."

Her smile blinded him. "Thank you, Carter. That's awesome." She jumped up. "I'll go change, and we'll get started."

After she left, he stared glumly at the water. Was he stupid? If he'd kept his mouth shut, Abby would still be beside him, sunbathing like a beautiful goddess, at arm's length.

Maybe his subconscious was trying to point out how self-destructive it would be to initiate a physical relationship under these circumstances. Even so, his libido demanded equal time. It was hours yet until sundown. Anything could happen.

Abby was thrilled and surprised that Carter had agreed to more on-camera time. She changed back into her clothes, twisted her damp hair into a loose knot on the back of her head and rushed to the great room to prepare for this next session. The fire, of course, had long since burned out.

Since she didn't have the heart to ask Carter to build another, she shifted his chair in front of some beautiful cherry bookcases. And she tossed a Native American blanket over the back corner of the chair.

By the time she had the scene prepared to her liking, Carter was back.

He had showered. Her twitching nose told her that. The scent of a very expensive aftershave emanated from him. Why would a man shave midafternoon? To be ready for a rendezvous later in the evening?

Her heart skipped a beat, but she focused on her work. "I'm all set," she said. "Why don't you take your seat, and we'll get started."

Carter was dressed a little less casually this time. His dark dress pants and gray knit polo shirt showcased his impressive physique. It was clear that the owner of Sunset Acres was a hands-on boss, one who spent plenty of time doing heavy chores and building up the strength to bench-press a car. Or woo a woman.

When she noticed he had chosen to go without shoes, she melted a little. Something about those large, tanned feet struck her as both masculine and boyish.

He smiled at her as he sprawled in the chair and ran his hands across his head. "I threw some potatoes in the oven. If we can wrap this up in forty-five minutes, I'll get the steaks on the grill. There's stuff in the fridge to make a salad, if you don't mind doing that."

"I'd be happy to." She peered through the camera and frowned. "I like you relaxed, but you've messed up your hair." Without overthinking it, she went to him and used her fingers to comb the thick, damp strands until she was happy with how he looked.

Carter took her arm and kissed the inside of her wrist. "I like it when you groom me, Abs."

She pursed her lips, refusing to let him see that one achingly tender kiss had her undone. "You mean like a gorilla mom with her baby?"

His jaw jutted. "I'm a full-grown man, Abby. You can count on that."

"Duly noted." She took her spot behind the camera. "Start with staff," she said calmly. "How many full-time employees do you have? What do they do? And what about seasonal and part-time?"

The camera started rolling, and Carter began talking. Despite Abby's total unfamiliarity with the topic, he managed to make it interesting. She quizzed him on herd sizes and breeds and what constituted a "good" year. She asked about weather disasters like tornadoes and hailstorms and fires, and then lesser crises like drought and floods.

The more Carter talked, the more Abby realized how deeply devoted he was to his heritage. He had to be. No one else loved it like he did.

Lastly, she touched on his family.

"They're actually coming for a visit this weekend," Carter said. "My parents, my sister and brother-in-law, and my niece, Beebee."

"Beebee?"

"They named her Beatrice, but that might stick when she's ten or eleven. At eight months, Beebee works."

Abby turned off the camera and stretched. "I have one last question, but I don't want it on camera."

He raised an eyebrow. "Oh? Should I be worried?"

"It's not about you. It's about the festival."

"Sounds serious from the tone of your voice."

Abby curled up on one end of the sofa and picked at a loose thread on the knee of her jeans. "I stumbled on something yesterday…something that might make a huge jumping-off point for my documentary. But I wanted to get your opinion."

"Go on…"

"When I was in the diner eating lunch, I overheard a conversation in the booth behind me. I wasn't eavesdropping on purpose, but it was hard not to listen. One woman was saying she heard someone stole a ton of money from the Soiree on the Bay checking account. Could that possibly be true? Nothing was mentioned in the meeting yesterday."

Carter scowled. "That's a dead end, Abby. We've talked about this. Royal thrives on innuendo and gossip. It grows as fast as kudzu. But ninety percent of the time, there's nothing to it. People don't like outsiders poking their noses in our business. You need to drop it. Find another angle. Otherwise, you'll end up alienating the very people who could help you with your project."

Abby was stunned by his vehemence. And hurt. The careless way he referred to her as an *outsider*, gave his warning a personal slant. Was that what he thought of her?

When Carter left to go put the steaks on the grill, she carried all her gear to the car and then wandered into the kitchen and began fixing a salad. As promised, she had everything at hand in the oversize, cutting-edge refrigerator. Finding a large bowl and a small pitcher for the dressing gave her an excuse to snoop through his cabinets.

As she worked, her pride still stung from his harsh rebuke. And her heart. Soiree on the Bay wouldn't be the first festival to be rocked by graft and greed. Local sponsors, both individual and corporate, had fronted an enormous amount of money to move the event forward.

Carter might not like it. In fact, she wouldn't bring it up again. But on her own, she was determined to explore this lead, tenuous though it was. Almost all gossip contained a grain of truth, no matter how tiny. She would follow this road until it petered out—or gave her the impetus she needed to put her documentary on a strong footing.

Abby didn't eat much red meat as a rule, but the steaks were extraordinary. She supposed a man who owned an enormous ranch learned early how to prepare beef. It was tender and subtly flavored. With the loaded baked potatoes and salad, it was the perfect meal.

Though Abby offered to help with cleanup, he refused. "There's not that much. And my housekeeper comes at ten in the morning."

"In that case, I should be getting back to town," she said.

Carter stilled, his back to her as he put things in the fridge. He shot her a look over his shoulder. "Or you could stay." The gleam in his beautiful blue eyes was temptation, pure and simple.

Here it was. Decision time. It would be much easier to get caught up in the moment, but Carter wasn't taking that tack. He was asking flat out. Offering her a clear choice. Be intimate with him, or choose to walk away.

He had given her everything she could ask for in terms of the interview. It was going to make incredibly good footage. But she felt no compunction to stay based on that. Whatever happened between the two of them was not going to be business.

The positives were clear. He was an honorable man, a conscientious son. A reputable landowner. Beyond that, he was sexy as hell. She knew without hesitation that he would be good to a woman in bed. Or *bad*, if she desired.

Up until this visit to Royal, Texas, she had been cautious in her love life. Her few relationships had been based on shared interests and a mutual desire for sexual satisfaction. But in every case, she had felt relief when the weeks or months were over, and she was *single* again. She'd told herself that she wasn't good at giving and receiving intimacy. Mostly, because she was too self-sufficient, too private.

Yet now, here was Carter. The man who burned away every last one of her reservations with a single look. Her body recognized him as a potential lover. But there was nothing simple about it. In fact, the urgency she felt was both astonishing and intimidating.

"Is that a good idea?" she asked, stalling for time to answer her own doubts.

"I could be convinced to come to the hotel with you." He leaned his hips against the counter and folded his arms across his chest. His face was hard to read.

She forced a laugh. "After you lectured me about Royal's gossipy grapevine? No, thanks. I don't want the whole town knowing what we do."

His expression softened. "It's your call, Abs. I won't be accused of pressuring you."

"I know that, dammit." She put her hands to her hot

cheeks, mortified. "I'm sorry." Perhaps this was where his extra decade gave him the edge. He'd probably lived this scene half a dozen more times than she had. She took a deep breath to steady her nerves. "I liked riding with you this morning. Could we take Foxtrot out for an evening cruise? I want to chase the sunset, hard and fast."

A flush rode high on his cheekbones. His eyes darkened. "We can do that. Meet me in the stable in fifteen minutes."

And then he was gone. Abby sought out the guest bathroom again and tidied her hair, securing it more tightly in its knot. As she stared at herself in the mirror, she wondered what Carter saw when he looked at her. Some men had called her exotic. It was a description she didn't really enjoy.

She didn't want to be different, at least not in that way. Though she had no hard data to back it up, her gut feeling was that Carter saw her as a woman first. A sexual being. A human with hopes and dreams.

She was okay with that. Because she recognized those same aspects in him. And something about him drew her like no one she had ever met.

It struck her suddenly, that not once had she entertained the idea of taking her camera on this outing. The professional Abby was done for the day. Tonight was all about *pleasure*.

As she walked through the house and out to the barn, she listed all the reasons not to stay with Carter. She had no clothes, no suitcase, nothing but a tube of Chap-Stick in her purse. Would she wake up in the morning feeling awkward and embarrassed? The answer was almost surely yes.

But even as she tried to talk herself out of tumbling into his bed, she knew the decision had been made.

The barn smelled amazing. As a city girl, she saw it as an anomaly, but one she liked. The atmosphere was earthy and real. When she saw the man waiting for her, her heart stumbled. He was wearing the Stetson this time. And riding boots.

The horse whinnied softly when Abby approached.

Carter smiled at her, an uncomplicated, straight-forward look that encompassed welcome and desire and forbidden promises.

"I'm putting you in front his time," he said.

Unlike before, there were no instructions. He simply put his hands on her waist and hefted her up into the saddle. His easy strength gave her a little thrill.

Moments later, he settled in behind her, his arms coming around her to hold the reins. His lips brushed the back of her neck. "You ready?"

It was a question with layers of meaning. "Yes," she answered, her response firm and unequivocal. "I can't wait."

Eight

Carter knew the exact moment Abby unwound. Like a rag doll, all the stiffness left her body, and her spine relaxed against his chest. He held the reins with one hand, so he could curl his arm around her waist.

The large saddle accommodated both of them comfortably. Foxtrot was a strong stallion, easily capable of bearing their weight and more. As the horse ambled away from the house toward the road, Carter told himself he had to concentrate. He had precious cargo. But all he wanted to do was bury his face in Abby's hair and hope she had stayed for more than an evening excursion on the ranch.

The sunset was particularly beautiful. Just enough clouds to make striking patterns of orange and pink and gold, much like the night he and Abby had first met. Already, that moment seemed like eons ago. But it wasn't, and he'd do well to remember that.

He nuzzled her ear. "You still want speed?"

She nodded. "Definitely."

He gave Foxtrot a nudge with his knees and felt the jolt of adrenaline as the powerful animal reached his stride. They were streaking down the road that bisected the ranch at a dizzying speed. It was a safe enough course.

Abby's delighted squeal made Carter smile. He pushed the horse faster and harder. Foxtrot loved the free rein. Even though it had been a hot day, at this hour and this speed, the wind felt chilly. He held Abby close, his posture protective.

Carter knew she was strong and independent, but she was young and new to Texas. He wouldn't let any*thing* or any*one* harm her, not even himself.

At last, they reached the far boundary of his acreage and turned around to head for home. Now Foxtrot's gallop was more sedate. Eventually, Carter slowed him further still. No point in ending the night too soon.

"Are you cold?" he asked.

"A little. But it's okay. I wouldn't have missed this."

"What would you be doing back in New York about now?"

He felt her shrug. "Maybe seeing a play. I adore Broadway. Always have. I actually thought about pursuing acting at one point."

"You'd have been good at it, I think. You have a very expressive face. And a beautiful voice."

She turned her head and rested her cheek over his

heart for a moment. "Thank you, Carter. That's a sweet thing to say."

"But true."

He held her close, steering the horse in the gathering gloom.

As they neared the house, Abby whispered something he didn't quite catch.

"What was that, Abs?"

Still facing straight ahead, she reached behind her and cupped his cheek with a slender, long-fingered hand. "I don't have any clean clothes with me. Or anything for that matter."

The insinuation went straight to his head and his groin. "I can hook you up," he said gruffly. "The guest bathroom has everything you'll need. And we can throw your clothes in the washer. I'll give you one of my shirts in the meantime."

She nodded. "Then I'd like to stay the night."

Things got fuzzy for Carter after that. He had wanted her for hours. The day had been one long and wonderful—but frustrating—dance of foreplay.

Now Abby was in his arms and committed to his bed. He'd won the lottery, though he would have sworn he wasn't a gambling man.

At the stable, he dismounted and helped her down. "I have to deal with the horse. If you'll wait for me, we can take a shower together."

In the illumination from the light inside the barn, her expression was bashful. "I think this first time I'd feel more comfortable getting ready on my own. Okay?"

He kissed her forehead. "Whatever you want." He

was still fixated on that one important phrase *this first time*. How many would there be? Abby had a job to do in Royal. She wouldn't be at his beck and call. And his days were plenty busy, too.

It was pointless to overanalyze things. He removed Foxtrot's saddle and rubbed him down before checking his food and water. Then he lowered the lights and closed up the barn. As he walked back to the house, he felt jittery. A shot of whiskey might be nice. But even that couldn't dull the hunger he felt.

When he reached his suite, the walk-in closet door stood open. Abby had clearly helped herself to an item of his clothing. That image kept him hard all during his shower. And when he returned to the bedroom and found her sitting cross-legged in the center of his bed, his erection grew.

She had picked out a plain white cotton button-down and had rolled the long sleeves to her elbows. Her dark, wavy hair fell around her shoulders. The shirttails covered her modestly.

But not for long…

Carter wore only a damp towel tucked around his hips. He had a hard time catching his breath. "Did you find everything you need?"

She tilted her head to one side and gave him a mischievous grin. "Not yet."

That was the thing that kept tripping him up. Abby Carmichael looked young and innocent, but she wasn't. She was an adult, with a woman's wants and needs. Luckily for him, she had found her way into his bed.

When he tossed the towel on a nearby chair, Abby

lost her smile. Her gaze settled on his sex. He saw the muscles in her throat move when she swallowed.

"Scoot over," he said, pulling the covers back and joining her. He sprawled on his side, propping his head on his hand. "You look beautiful, Ms. Carmichael. And you smell delicious."

Abby didn't move. He thought she might be holding her breath. Finally, she exhaled a little puff of air. "Your guest bathroom is stocked with lovely toiletries."

"I'm glad you approve." He ran his thumb across her exposed knee. "Are you scared of me, Abby?"

She wrinkled her nose. "No. My birth control pills are at the hotel. You'll have to wear a condom."

"That's not a problem." He slid his hand from her knee to her thigh, under the shirt. "Talk to me, Abs."

Her hands were clasped in her lap. She looked either nervous or uncertain, or both. "I haven't slept with a lot of men," she admitted. "And you're not like any of them."

"Meaning what?"

"What if this doesn't work? I've known you four days. That's not me, Carter. I'm not an impulsive kind of woman. But this chemistry between us…it's…"

"Undeniable? Explosive? Breath-stealing?"

She nodded. "All those things."

He sat up and leaned against the headboard, pulling her into a loose embrace, combing his fingers through her hair. "We'll take it slow. You tell me if I do something you don't like."

She pulled back and stared at him with those deep

brown eyes framed in thick lashes. "I don't think that's going to be a problem."

With unsteady hands, he unbuttoned the shirt Abby wore, *his* shirt, gradually revealing pale brown skin that was soft and smooth and begging for his kisses. Her breasts were high and full, the tips a lighter shade than her eyes.

When he managed the final button, he slid the garment off her slender body and cast it aside. Abby watched him with a rapt expression that stoked the flame burning inside him. When he palmed her breast, she gasped.

He thumbed the nipple, watching in fascination as it furled tightly. When he leaned down to take that bud into his mouth, Abby's choked moan ignited him. He dragged her onto the mattress and lifted himself over her, giving the other breast equal attention.

Her hands fisted in his hair painfully. He suspected they were both too primed to make this last as long as he wanted, but he was going to try.

She moved restlessly as he kissed her forehead, her eyelids, her nose and finally, her soft lips. The taste of her was like a drug, clouding his brain. "Abby," he groaned.

They kissed wildly, like they had in the pool. Only now, they were in a big soft bed made for a man and a woman. And pleasure. *Endless* pleasure.

He lost himself in the kissing, his hands equally occupied learning the hills and valleys of her lithe, long-limbed body. She was soft and strong, a seductive combo.

In some dim, conscious corner of his brain, he remembered protection. Rolling away from her, he snatched open a drawer and found what he wanted. After ripping open the package, he sheathed himself, knowing he couldn't hold out very long this first time.

When he delicately stroked Abby's center, she was warm and wet and ready for him. He entered her with two fingers, feeling her body tighten against his intrusion. "I need you, Abs. I'll make it up to you, I swear."

Even then, he waited, stroking that tiny bundle of nerves that controlled her pleasure until she arched off the bed and cried out.

He entered her then with one forceful push, feeling her inner muscles contract around him, her body still in the throes of sweet release. The sensation was indescribable. He was consumed with lust and racked with the need to give her tenderness and passion in equal measure.

As he moved in her slowly, Abby squirmed beneath him, locking her legs around his waist and angling her lower body so they fit together perfectly. She was dreamy-eyed, flushed, her skin damp and hot.

"Don't hold back, Carter. I want it all."

Her words were a demand, one he was happy to meet. His world narrowed to her face. Each time he pumped his hips, he saw her react. The flutter of long-lashed eyelids, the small gasps of breath, the way her chin lifted toward the ceiling and her lips parted as she reached for a second climax.

She found it as he found his. He came for eons, it seemed, shuddering against her and whispering her name. When it was over, he slumped on top of her, barely managing to brace most of his weight on his elbows.

He might have dozed.

When reality finally intruded, it was because Abby squirmed out from under him to go to the bathroom. Carter rolled to his back and slung one arm over his face. He felt blissfully sated, but oddly unsettled.

Some things were too good to be true, and this might be one of them. Madeline hadn't been the woman for him. He could see that now with the benefit of hindsight. Losing her had wounded his pride and his dignity. The broken relationship left him lonely and afraid to trust.

Abby wasn't Madeline. Carter knew that. But she was no more likely to hang around, so he needed to keep his head out of his ass and be smart about this.

While his lover was still occupied, he crawled out of bed and retrieved her clothes from the guest bathroom. As he turned on the washing machine and added soap, he stared at the bra and panties in his hands. They looked alien.

This was a male household.

He'd had a handful of one-night stands since his aborted engagement. Mostly out of town. Almost exclusively with sophisticated women who took what they wanted and asked for nothing in return.

Abby was different. Honestly, he couldn't say exactly how or why, but he felt it in his gut. The fact that confusion swirled in his brain warned him to take a step back.

He tossed the few items of laundry into the water

and closed the lid. She was spending the night. There was nothing he could do about that. So, he might as well enjoy himself.

Abby was tucked up in his bed, snug beneath the covers when he returned to his room. The sight of her constricted his chest.

She raised up on her elbow. "Where did you go?"

"I promised to wash your clothes, remember?"

"Oh. Right. I was thinking about leaving in a little bit, but I guess I won't."

He frowned. "Leaving? Why?"

Abby shoved the hair from her face, some of it still damp. Her gaze was guarded. "You'll need to be up early in the morning. And I've already taken a lot of your time this week. I don't want to overstay my welcome."

Was there a note of hurt in that explanation? Had she picked up on his unease? Guilt swamped him. He climbed back into bed, pulling her close. "I'll let you know if you're in the way, Abs. For now, we're right where we should be."

They slept for an hour, or maybe two. Then he made love to her again. This time was less frantic, but no less stunning. He wasn't a teenager anymore. Sex was an important part of life, but it hadn't been the driving force in the last few years.

Now he craved her with a fiery intensity that took his breath away. What was he going to do about that?

When he roused the next time, he stumbled down the hall to put her clothes in the dryer. He contemplated *forgetting*, so she would have to stay longer. But he knew she had an interview lined up with Billy Holmes, and Carter couldn't be the one to sabotage her project, even if he wasn't keen on knowing Abby would be alone with Holmes.

Sometime before dawn, he awakened to the pleasant sensation of female fingers wrapped around his erection.

Abby nuzzled her face in the crook of his neck. "It will be morning soon. Are you up for one more round before I go?"

He cleared his throat, feeling like a sailor lost at sea. The only thing he could hang on to was Abby. "I think you know the answer to that."

He took care of protection once again, and Abby climbed on top with no apparent self-consciousness. Cupping her firm, rounded ass in his hands, he thrust into her warmth, feeling his certainty slip away.

Were there some things a man could make exceptions for? Some prizes worth any price? His life was all mapped out. It was a *good* life. But there was no room for self-indulgence. Abby was cotton candy at the fair, a brilliant display of fireworks on a hot summer night. But she wasn't the mundane day-to-day of responsibility.

When she leaned down to steal a kiss—her hair cocooning them in intimacy—he quickly lost the desire for self-reflection. Her breasts danced in front of him, ripe for the tasting. He took every advantage.

Her body was a mystery and a wonder of divine engineering. This was the third time he'd taken her tonight. He should have been sated and tired. Instead, he felt invincible.

When she cried out and came, he rolled her to her back and pounded his way to the finish line, shocked even now at the effect she had on him. Was it some kind of sorcery? Or was he simply sex deprived?

Maybe there was yet another explanation he didn't want to acknowledge.

He had slept only in snatches the entire night. This time, he fell hard and deep into unconsciousness. When his alarm went off at seven, one side of the bed was cool and empty, and his lover was gone.

Abby yawned her way through a hotel breakfast in the dining room. The eggs and bacon, fresh fruit and croissants were delightful, but she didn't enjoy the meal as much as she should have. She felt disheveled and gloomy, and she didn't have the luxury of going to her room and crashing.

Billy Holmes was expecting her at eleven.

She refused to think about Carter at all. He confused her. That was the last thing she needed right now. Her documentary was still an unfocused blob. She *had* to find a sound angle if she hoped to make any progress at all.

By the time she had showered and changed into a melon-colored pantsuit with a jaunty aqua and coral scarf around her throat, she felt a renewed determination. The fashionable clothes were intentional. This documentary was her big shot. She had someone at a major studio willing to take a chance on her. The film she produced had to be rock-solid. And it didn't hurt to dress for success.

Driving out to the Edmonds' property steadied her. As she passed an ornate sign that read Elegance Ranch, she wrinkled her nose. The name was pretentious, at least to her. Billy had texted her a set of directions. That was a good thing, because the sprawling private dynasty included a pool and stables and several guesthouses in addition to the massive, luxurious main house.

She recalled from the meeting at the Texas Cattleman's Club that Rusty Edmond, the oft-married but now-single patriarch, lived there along with his son, Ross, daughter, Gina, and stepson, Asher. And for a reason yet to be discovered, Billy Holmes lived in one of the guest cottages.

The property was completely private, surrounded by miles of ranch land. Abby stopped several times to get out and photograph interesting spots. Once she was cleared at the gatehouse, there were no other impediments. She had allowed herself plenty of extra time. Being prompt was one of her personal mantras.

By the time she located Billy's guesthouse, her nerves returned. His home was beautiful, lushly landscaped and neither huge nor tiny. How had he ended up here? And why had the family accepted him as one of their own?

When Abby rang the doorbell, a uniformed older woman with gray hair answered. "You must be Ms. Carmichael," she said. "Please come in. Mr. Holmes is expecting you."

Abby followed the woman through the house to a pleasant sunroom overlooking a grassy, well-manicured lawn.

Billy Holmes stood. "Abby. Right on time. So glad you could join me. Would you like a drink?"

"Water for me, please."

He offered her a comfortable seat and took an adjoining chair. "How are you liking Royal, so far?"

"I'm getting my bearings," she said diplomatically. "The people are friendly. And I enjoyed the advisory council meeting." She set her glass of water aside. "Would you mind if I go ahead and get set up to film our conversation? I don't want to miss anything. Unless the camera makes you uncomfortable."

"The camera doesn't bother me at all," he said, giving her a smile that was almost too charming.

Fortunately for Abby, Holmes's phone dinged. He stood and dealt with the text, leaving her a few moments to frame a backdrop and get her equipment where she wanted it. By the time she was ready, Billy returned.

She motioned to where she had situated a chair adjacent to a large-paned window. "May we get started?"

"Of course." He put his phone in the breast pocket of his jacket and unbuttoned the coat before sitting down. With the sun gilding his dark hair and his deliberately scruffy five-o'clock shadow, Billy Holmes looked every inch the bad boy.

Abby sighted her subject through the viewfinder one last time and then stepped back. "How long have you lived in Royal, Mr. Holmes?"

"Call me Billy, please. I guess it's been two and a half years now. Time flies."

"And what is your connection to the Edmond family?" she asked.

"Ross and I were college buddies. He always talked about Royal and how much he loved it. When I decided to relocate and get settled for good, I thought about Maverick County as an option. Ross offered me one of the guesthouses, and here I am."

"He sounds like a very good friend," Abby remarked.

"Indeed."

"Who came up with the festival idea originally? Was it you?"

His smile was modest. "Hard to say. Ross and Gina and Asher and I were talking one day about ways to put Royal on the map. It was a brainstorming session, a group project."

"What do you hope to achieve? The actual festival site is a long way from here."

He shrugged. "Distance is nothing in Texas. Royal will be the jumping-off point for the festival. Our main focus is luxury, whether it's food or wine or music or art. We're marketing to a particular clientele. No empty beer bottles and smelly port-a-johns. Beyond that, we want to bring people together, and also raise significant money for charity." He cleared his throat. "To that end, we're sparing no expense. We want Soiree on the Bay to be talked about for years to come."

Abby kept asking him questions for another half hour and then began winding down the narrative. Billy Holmes was good on camera, charismatic, easy to listen to… This footage would be excellent.

Before she wrapped up, she decided to take a risk. "I heard a rumor in town," she murmured, keeping her tone light. "Something about money missing from the festival account. Could you comment on that?"

Billy's expression changed from affable to calculating. He seemed tense. "Turn off the camera."

"Of course."

After she did as he demanded, Billy stood and paced, his face flushed. "Off the record? Yes, that's true. Ross discovered the discrepancy. But it's a family matter. We're handling it."

Yet Billy Holmes *wasn't* family. "I see." She didn't see at all, but she was stalling. "Is the festival in danger?"

"Of course not," he snapped. "We're full steam ahead. It's going to be epic."

Abby realized she wasn't going to get anything further out of Billy Holmes. If he had slipped before, now he was covering his tracks.

In the end, she was forced to put her equipment away and sit through a long and one-sided lunch conversation. Holmes liked talking about himself. That much was clear.

But he was being closemouthed on the topic that interested her most.

Only the housekeeper's culinary skills made the meal memorable. The quiche lorraine was amazing, as was the caprese salad.

Eventually, Abby decided she had stayed long enough not to seem rude if she bolted. "I should get back to town," she said. "Thanks so much for lunch and the interview."

Holmes stood when she did. "My pleasure." His expression was guarded now, as if he was aware he had overstepped some boundary and now regretted his candor.

He walked her to the front door and out to her car, helping carry one of her bags. Abby had left her sunglasses in the glove box. She shielded her eyes with her hand. "One other thing. I'd love to speak with a few of the charities who will benefit from the Soiree. Could you make that happen?" She was deliberately playing to his vanity.

"Of course." He preened. "You should start with Valencia Donovan at Donovan Horse Rescue. You'll like her. She has an interesting story to tell."

"Perfect," Abby said. "You'll give her my number? See if she's willing to be interviewed? I don't want to assume…"

"I'll deal with it this afternoon. If you're lucky, she might be able to see you tomorrow."

Nine

Abby was thrilled that the wheels were beginning to turn more quickly with regard to her documentary, but even so, she couldn't stop thinking about Carter. She'd written him a polite but brief note that morning, explaining that she had a busy day ahead.

What did he think when he found her gone? Was he disappointed?

Maybe he was glad. Some men didn't like complications.

When she got back to the hotel, she forced herself to concentrate on work. Between the brief footage she had shot during the advisory board meeting and the personal interviews with Carter Crane and Billy Holmes, she already had a great start. Now came the hard part of scrolling through frames and editing the sequences she knew would serve her purpose.

Billy Holmes was as good as his word, apparently. Abby got a text midafternoon from Valencia Donovan inviting her to meet Valencia and see her charity at ten tomorrow morning. That should work. After responding in the affirmative, Abby was soon deep into her storyboard. What was the hook going to be? More and more, she was convinced it was the money trail.

When her stomach growled, she was surprised to realize it was after seven. Sitting in the restaurant didn't appeal, so she ordered room service. That way she could continue working while she ate.

Two hours later, she stood and stretched. She'd made good progress. Now she could goof off and watch TV or add some new shots to her Instagram account. As a budding filmmaker, social media was essential.

She was just about to get in the shower when her phone dinged. It was Carter. Her pulse skittered. What did he want? She snatched up her cell and read the text.

Abby—Hope you had a good day. How about coming out to the ranch for dinner tomorrow night? I know my family would love to meet you. Let me know…

In the bathroom mirror, her expression was startled. Meet his *family*? Why? She scowled at her reflection, parsing his words for hidden meanings. Maybe the invitation was no more or less than it seemed. After all, not all families got along perfectly. Maybe Carter thought an outsider would cushion any squabbles.

She didn't answer right away. During her shower, she tried not to think about Carter's offer to *shower* together at his house. She had turned him down. Maybe now she regretted that. Would he have made love to her then? And again in the bed?

Thinking about sex with Carter made her hot and bothered. By the time she dried off and put on a clean T-shirt and sleep pants, she was no closer to knowing what to do.

She liked Carter Crane. A lot. He was funny and smart, and so sexy she had let him coax her into bed with embarrassing ease.

That was what worried her. If she had so little self-control around the man, wouldn't it be safer to keep her distance? This town wasn't for her. Neither was this lifestyle. She liked being free and able to go wherever the wind took her.

If she embarked on a relationship with one of Royal's premier bachelors, wasn't it possible she could end up getting hurt?

In the end, she chickened out. Her text was a monument to indecision.

Carter—I'm not sure about my schedule tomorrow. I should be able to let you know by noon. Okay???

She hit Send and tucked her phone under a pillow, too anxious to wait for his answer. Although she was finished with work for the evening, she couldn't resist taking another look at the interview with Carter. She uploaded some of the raw footage to her laptop and un-muted the sound.

Like most people, she didn't enjoy hearing her own voice. But Carter's made up for it. The timbre of his speech was intensely masculine. He looked straight at the lens, unflinching. Though he claimed to have no experience being on camera, he came across as natural and appealing. Even someone with no interest in cattle and horses would find his enthusiasm compelling.

It didn't hurt that his rugged good looks played well.

Finally, she shut off the electronics and did a few half-hearted yoga stretches. Her usual routine had been shot to heck. She was supposed to be finding a revelation or two. About Soiree on the Bay. Or ranchers in general. Or the Texas Cattleman's Club way of life.

Instead, Texas was showing her a few truths about herself.

The next morning, she hopped out of bed, refusing to think about hot, sexy ranchers and wild, incredible sex. She grabbed a croissant and coffee downstairs before bolting to her rental car. Valencia Donovan's property was a few miles outside of town, but Abby wasn't sure how far out.

In the end, she made it with ten minutes to spare. Valencia met her at the gate with a friendly smile. "Hi, Abby," she said. "Billy filled me in about your work. How exciting. I'd love to have my organization featured in your documentary."

Valencia was gorgeous. Her eyes were the same brown as Abby's, but the comparison ended there. She was tall and leggy with a mane of wavy, golden blond hair. Her skinny jeans and multicolored peasant blouse painted a picture of free-spirited warmth.

Abby felt a little dowdy in comparison, which was dumb, because she had been perfectly satisfied with her appearance when she left the hotel. Perhaps something about Valencia was an unpleasant reminder of all the blond and perfect girls who had at times made her life a misery growing up.

In reality, Valencia was nothing but welcoming and complimentary of Abby's chosen profession and everything else. She was patient while Abby filmed various aspects of the horse rescue. After they toured the barn and met a few of the horses, the other woman sighed. "I'm in the mood for some of Amanda Battle's lemon meringue pie. What if we head back to town and finish our conversation at the diner?"

"I'm game," Abby said.

Over lunch, the two of them bonded. Valencia was funny and unpretentious. Abby learned that she had left a successful corporate career to rescue horses.

Abby took a sip of her tea. "From boardroom to horse ranch? What was the appeal?"

"I love horses, always have," Valencia said. "I had saved up enough money to buy the land, and I've begun locating horses in peril. You'd be shocked how many people think they want to own a horse and then find out how much hard work it is."

"But not Royal ranchers."

"Oh, no. The horses I rescue come from all over. I sometimes drive five or six hours to pick up an animal."

"Impressive. I don't mean to be rude, but are there enough people who care about mistreated horses to donate to a charity? Billy Holmes told me that Donovan Horse Rescue is one of the beneficiaries of Soiree on the Bay."

"I'm hoping to make the focus of my work equine therapy, in particular for children. You see, I'm very interested in providing immersive summer camp opportunities, and kids who have experienced tragedy respond well to horses. Particularly when part of their activities include learning how to care for an animal. Feeding, brushing, that sort of thing… I filled out an application and submitted it to the festival board. They must have liked my pitch."

"Do you mind if I ask how much you're going to receive?"

"Not at all." Valencia named a number in the high five figures.

"Wow! You must be very excited."

"I definitely am. I've been working on my business plan. Of course, I won't receive any money until all the ticket sales are in. But in the meantime, I'm getting everything ready on paper, so I don't miss a single moment. I'm thrilled that I was chosen."

"I see why." Abby flashed her a warm smile. "You're passionate about this project, and I'm sure that came across in your proposal. Good for you. I think it's wonderful that the money from the festival will get you started. And to know that children will benefit? You must be very proud."

Back at the hotel, Abby studied the notes she'd made

during lunch. She had filmed Valencia speaking in the barn. But the footage of the horse rescue operation would be excellent B-roll. No one wanted to see a documentary that was only talking heads. Abby's narration would flesh out the woman's vision.

At one thirty, she stared at her phone, wishing she could pretend she had never seen last night's communication from Carter. If he'd sent a simple "let's hook up" text, it might have been easier to answer. She could have responded from the standpoint of purely physical gratification, nothing more. But if she went out to Sunset Acres this afternoon, she would have to interact with his family.

It didn't make sense. She knew without a doubt that Carter wasn't making a grand meet-the-parents gesture. Abby had known him less than a week. So why had he invited her at all?

The clock was ticking. To wait any longer would be unforgivably rude.

Gnawing her lip, she tapped out a long-overdue reply.

Is the offer still good? I finished up a couple of things earlier than expected.

One minute passed. Then two. When the phone finally dinged, she exhaled all the breath she had been holding. Carter's reply was not nuanced at all, darn it. No lines to read between.

Sure. Why don't you show up around five? We'll eat at six. Or I can pick you up, if you don't want to drive.

Abby was alarmed to realize how much relief she experienced.

I'll see you then...happy to drive. Can I bring anything?

Carter posted a smiley face.

You're staying in a hotel. I think that gives you a free pass. See you soon...

Abby clicked out of the text screen. Now her next question was very personal. Should she pack a bag? If she *didn't*, she'd be giving her libido a clear signal. That this was dinner. Nothing more.

On the other hand, if Carter was interested in a repeat performance of *Abby and Carter's Greatest Hits*, she would be much more comfortable with her own toiletries and a change of clothes.

Did a grown man invite his lover to spend the night when his parents were in residence? Of course, Carter *had* made a point of mentioning a guesthouse and his privacy.

On the other hand, was Abby really his lover? That sounded like a far more formal relationship than what she had with him.

They had slept together. True. But that was it. Or was it?

She changed her mind about what to wear half a dozen times. It was hot today, scorching really. In this weather, she always preferred a light, loose-fitting dress. Fortunately she had one she hadn't worn yet.

The double layer of white gauzy fabric and halter neck meant she wouldn't even have to wear a bra.

That seemed like a prudent choice when the temps were nearing the hundred-degree mark. The dress had its own woven, gold leather belt. She had sandals to match. And a pair of unabashedly over-the-top dangly gold earrings.

Because she was antsy, she got ready far too early. She decided to leave anyway and drive around town before heading out to the ranch. Her camera would be in the trunk, just in case.

Friday night in Royal meant a lot of people in town. Restaurants and bars were hopping, even at this early hour. Teenagers thronged the streets, doing all the silly things adolescents do when it's summertime, and hormones are raging.

Abby had to smile. Some behaviors were universal. She hadn't dated much in high school, but she'd suffered through a couple of unrequited crushes. It had been college before she had really come out of her shell. She'd been shy by nature and inclined to stay out of the spotlight.

That was one reason filmmaking appealed to her. She could control the narrative. No one would be staring at her as long as she stayed behind the camera.

Finally, she turned the car in the direction of Carter's ranch, smiling as she recalled their first encounter. Even now, the memory of him on horseback—silhouetted against the sun—caused her heart to beat faster.

This evening's visit to Sunset Acres made her uneasy, and she wasn't even there yet. Despite their night of unbridled sex, much of her contact with Carter up until now had been couched in terms of her project. Nothing about this latest invitation was business related.

It felt *personal*.

The last time she had seen him, he'd been asleep— his big, tanned body sprawled against white sheets, his hair mussed and his face unshaven. She had tiptoed out at the first hint of dawn, not wanting a confrontation. Cowardly? Sure. But an action and a choice predicated on self-preservation.

This time, she didn't linger anywhere on the property. She drove straight to Carter's house and parked. As she stepped out of the car, a curvy brunette with a baby on her hip came down the steps. "Hey there. You must be Abby. I'm Denise, Carter's younger sister. And this is Beebee."

Abby gazed at the infant with something like awe. Beebee was solid, her legs bracketed in rolls of baby fat. "Hi, Beebee."

The kid babbled a few nonsense syllables, but she didn't smile. Maybe she didn't approve of women who wanted to travel the world instead of getting pregnant.

Denise retrieved a plastic booster seat from her car, the kind that could be strapped to a chair. "Come on in, Abby. I want you to meet my husband and my mother. Dad is out back grilling with Carter."

Abby fell into step. "That must be a macho Texas guy thing. Grilling? I guess it's a requirement?"

Abby held open the door as Denise replied, "Not gonna lie. It's in their DNA. After all, this is beef country. At least Mom and I have convinced them to branch out over the years. There will be steaks, always, but chicken breasts, too, and fresh veggies."

"Sounds delicious." Abby's stomach growled. She'd gone easy at lunch, but now the smells wafting from the grill teased her taste buds.

Mrs. Crane was in the dining room. She was in her midfifties, attractive and fit. Carter's mom seemed pleasant enough, but Abby had the feeling that she was being assessed by her de facto hostess and maybe falling short.

The older woman grilled Abby right away. "So how long has my son known you, Ms. Carmichael?"

"Call me Abby, please. Not long at all. I've come to Royal to do a documentary on the Soiree on the Bay festival."

"Ah. But Carter has no interest in the festival."

"No, ma'am. None. But he's allowing me to film here at the ranch, so that I can showcase Royal and the ranching industry as a backdrop to my story."

"I see."

"Mama." Denise raised an eyebrow. "Behave."

Her mother gave her an innocent look. "I'm just getting to know Abby."

"Right." Denise shook her head, apparently used to her mother's tactics. She handed Beebee to the only other person in the room. "This is my husband, Ernie. Ernie, Abby."

Abby shook the man's free hand. "Nice to meet you. Your daughter is a sweetheart."

Ernie was quiet and seemed not to mind when his

little one yanked handfuls of his hair. "She keeps us on our toes," he said ruefully.

Mrs. Crane's given name was Cynthia, as Abby learned when the father-son duo came in bearing a platter of shrimp, the ubiquitous steak and chicken breasts.

When Carter's gaze met hers across the room, the jolt of heat was so profound, she looked around to see if anyone had noticed. Apparently not.

Carter smiled at the room in general, though his introduction was more personal. "Abby, this is my dad, Lamar. I see you've met the rest of the clan."

"I did," she said, taking the seat Denise offered her. Cynthia had set the table earlier while her son-in-law poured drinks. Abby was surprised to see that the menu was free of any alcoholic beverages. Only tea and iced coffee and lemonade were offered.

Denise whispered an explanation. "Daddy's a teetotaler now. Doctor's orders. He's supposed to be avoiding red meat, too, but that won't happen tonight."

There were no formalities observed, though everyone was dressed nicely, and nary a paper plate in sight. Cynthia had used china and crystal and a heavy, ornate silver service adorned with the letter *C*.

Abby wondered if the Cranes always dined so elegantly or if this show was for her benefit. No one seemed to think it odd that she was in attendance. But the longer the dinner lasted, the more she wondered why she had been included.

Conversation flowed freely. Abby was questioned at length about her job and her background and whether or not she watched college sports.

Cynthia pressed delicately at times, but finally with a vein of determination. "Tell us about your family, dear."

All eyes shifted to Abby. She set down her glass of iced tea and managed a smile, even though she might as well have been on the witness stand. "I'm an only child," she said. "My parents have been divorced for a very long time, though they are on good terms. Daddy is a filmmaker out in California. My mother works at Sotheby's in New York. Her specialty is appraising twentieth-century paintings."

"Impressive." Cynthia's gaze was assessing, as though trying to read between the lines. "And is this your first trip to Texas?"

"Yes, ma'am." Abby fell into old habits. Carter's mother was a force to be reckoned with, even though his father was a big ole teddy bear.

Denise chimed in. "And what do you think of Maverick County?"

A hushed silence fell over the room. Abby frowned inwardly. This was weird. "Um, it's very different from what I'm used to. But it has a beauty all its own, I suppose."

Ernie laughed, his kind eyes dancing. "Good for you, Abby. Stand up for yourself. This family is a bit much. Diplomacy is a required skill."

There was a momentary lull in the conversation. Denise and Cynthia left the table to serve dessert. Carter's sister had made two apple pies. Apparently, both Crane women were homemakers extraordinaire.

The remainder of the meal passed without incident. Abby noticed that Carter didn't have a whole lot to say in the midst of his boisterous family. Of course, the baby kept things lively, but even so, Carter's quiet presence was notable. He smiled a lot. And he answered when spoken to. Still, he seemed more watchful than anything else.

At last, Beebee fell asleep on her father's shoulder. Denise smiled. "We should head for the guesthouse soon. Mom, Dad…you stay as long as you want."

Cynthia gave her son a pointed look. "May I speak with you in the kitchen, Carter?"

Abby breathed a sigh of relief. The other members of his family were far less frightening.

But Denise unwittingly put a confrontation in motion. She scooped up Beebee and glanced at Abby. "Would you mind helping me change her into pajamas? Daddy and Ernie are dying to have another slice of pie without Mom noticing."

"Of course." Abby stood and followed the other woman down the hallway. They were heading away from the kitchen. But apparently, Carter and his mother had chosen to go to the sunroom instead.

Suddenly, Denise held up her hand and backed up. But it was too late. The conversation was impossible to ignore.

Cynthia's voice carried. "Why did you invite that girl tonight, Carter? What are you up to? Is this another doomed romantic alliance?"

Carter's tone was perfectly calm. "Abby is not a prospective fiancée. We're friends. I thought she might enjoy meeting my family. That's all."

"Bull testicles," his mother snapped. "You're playing games. But I must say that this one is better than your wretched *Madeline*."

Carter's reply was less conciliatory now. "At least you're being honest. It might have been nice if *one* of you told me you didn't like Madeline. I didn't find out until it was all over that my nearest and dearest had reservations about her."

"We didn't want to meddle."

"Since when?"

Abby's whole body was one big blush. She touched Denise on the arm. "I'm going to step outside for a few minutes. Please make my excuses."

Before Carter's sister could reply, Abby darted back the way she had come. She dodged the dining room and sneaked out onto the veranda and down to the driveway. In the dark, she put her hands to her hot cheeks. What had Carter been thinking? She was humiliated and confused.

After fifteen minutes, she knew she couldn't stay outside any longer without causing comment. She grabbed a thin sweater from the front seat of her car as an excuse and started to walk back inside.

As she hit the top step and took a breath for courage, the door opened suddenly. A familiar voice spoke out of the darkness.

"There you are," Carter said. "I was starting to worry about you."

Ten

Carter was pissed and frustrated. He loved his parents, but his mother could be a handful. Thankfully, Denise had whispered a heads-up to him, warning that she and Abby had unwittingly overheard the conversation between mother and son.

He turned on the porch light and saw Abby freeze when she realized it was him. "I just came to get my sweater out of the car," she said.

"No. You overheard my conversation with my mother, and you were embarrassed. I'm sorry, Abby."

He couldn't read her expression, but her body language spoke volumes. Her arms were wrapped tightly around her waist, and she had backed up as far as humanly possible without falling off the porch.

She placed her sweater with exaggerated care on the

railing. "Why did you invite me to come here tonight, Carter?" she asked.

The slight tremor in her voice made him feel like scum.

"Two reasons. First of all, I wanted to see you."

"And the second?"

"I haven't socialized much since Madeline called off the wedding," he admitted. "My mother is constantly on my case to *get back out there*. So I thought if she met you, I'd get credit for dating but she wouldn't pressure me, because she wouldn't approve of our relationship."

Abby's shock was visible. "Why not? I'm delightful."

He chuckled, charmed by her candor. "I won't argue with that. You definitely are. My mother, though, doesn't see you as ranch wife material. Sunset Acres means everything to my parents, even though they've handed it over to me. They know the kinds of sacrifices that are required, because they've made those very same sacrifices."

After a few beats of silence, Abby took a step toward him and exhaled audibly. "Not that I have any interest in marrying you or having your babies, Carter Crane, but why am I not ranch wife material?"

He stepped closer, as well, reaching out to brush his thumb over her cheek. "You don't even *like* Texas, Abs. There's nothing wrong with that, but it means my mother won't start making wedding plans. That's a good thing."

"Ah."

"I didn't think she would react so strongly tonight."

He grimaced. "Usually there's a honeymoon period before she starts vetting my female companions."

"Aren't you kind of old to have your mommy picking out your lovers?"

He pressed the heel of his hand to his forehead where a headache hammered. "You would think so, yes."

Abby cocked her head and gave him a steady stare that made him want to fidget. "I'm sure we should get back inside," she said. "I don't want to be rude."

"Why not? My family certainly hasn't been kind to *you* this evening."

"That's not entirely true. Denise and Ernie and the baby were pleasant. Your dad's a peach. And to be honest, your mother wasn't technically rude to me. In fact, you're the one who set this train wreck in motion."

He curled a strand of her hair around his finger. "I'll make it up to you, Abs, I swear. You look beautiful tonight by the way." His throat tightened as his body hardened. Her scent, something light and floral, teased his nostrils. "Are you wearing anything under that spectacular dress? I've been wondering all evening."

When she rested her cheek against his chest, his heart bumped against his rib cage. "That's on a need-to-know basis."

He held Abby close, linking both arms around her bare back, resting his chin on top of her head, feeling her slender body and feminine curves nestled against his flatter, harder frame. "I need to know," he said huskily. "Really, I do."

"Feel free to explore," she whispered.

It was a dangerous game they played. But he was

counting on his family's guilt to give him a few moments of privacy.

Slowly, he gathered Abby's skirt in two hands, pulling it upward until his fingers brushed her bare ass. Well, not entirely bare. She wore a tiny, lacy pair of panties that barely merited a mention.

His mouth went dry. He stroked her butt cheeks, feeling the smooth skin and taut flesh. As caresses went, it was mostly innocent. He didn't trespass anywhere he shouldn't. "That answers half the question," he groaned, wondering why the hell he had started this adventure with his whole damn family close at hand.

Abby slid her arms around his neck and looked up at him with a tiny smile on her face, one that mocked his handling of the evening. "You could kiss me," she said.

The last time they were together, he had been driven by hunger and adrenaline. Tonight, he was no less hungry, but he had more control. He kissed her deeply, holding her chin with two fingers and tracing the seam of her lips with his tongue, giving her passion wrapped in tenderness.

The kiss could have stayed that way, but Abby groaned and went up on her tiptoes to take what she wanted, reminding him that she was no shrinking violet waiting for him to direct her. She was passionate and needy and generous with her kisses.

His head swam. Though the hour was late, the humid air made his body damp and hot. He wanted to strip her naked and swim with her nude.

That image broke the last ounce of control he had over his baser impulses. "God, Abby." He dragged her closer still and ravaged her mouth. Sliding one hand beneath the top of her dress, he found a bare breast. The soft skin and pert tip were a fascinating contrast.

He was rapidly reaching a point of no return. With a muttered curse, he released her and stepped back. "Did I ruin your lipstick?"

"I'm not wearing any." She reached in her pocket and pulled out a clear lip gloss, using it to soothe lips that were puffy from his kisses.

Carter winnowed his fingers through her hair, tidying away the look of passion. "We have to go back in. They won't leave until we do."

"Okay."

He couldn't blame her for the lack of enthusiasm. "I'm sorry I made you uncomfortable tonight. It won't happen again, I swear."

She wrinkled her nose. "Don't make promises you can't keep."

As he started to open the door, she tugged on his arm. "One more thing. I haven't talked to you since I interviewed Billy Holmes."

His hackles went up. "What did he do?" Something in her voice made him wonder if there had been an incident.

"Not a thing. He was a perfect gentleman. But at the end of our meeting, I told him the rumor I had overheard… about the missing money."

"Oh, geez, Abby. I told you not to poke around in that. Was he angry?"

"Actually, he said it was true."

The smug look on her face didn't even bother Carter. He was too stunned. "You can't be serious."

"The camera was off. He lowered his voice and said it was a family matter, and that it was being handled."

Carter shook his head slowly. "I have a bad feeling about this. Who on the committee is handling the actual money part of the festival?"

"Asher, I think. But he's rich. Why would he need to skim funds?"

"I don't like you messing around in this, Abby. People get squirrelly when money is involved. You could be getting yourself into a dangerous situation."

"Or," she said, excitement lighting her face, "I could have found the focus for my documentary. An exposé. It doesn't get better than that!"

He ground his jaw. "Promise me you will let this go." He didn't want to quarrel with her, but he was certain his fears were well-founded.

Abby frowned at him. "Why are you so angry?"

"I'm not angry," he bit out. "I'm aggravated." And it was true. His feelings about Abby and his family and the festival coalesced into a fiery ball of sexual frustration that churned in his gut.

Carter yanked her close, lifting her off her feet and kissing her again. He held her tightly, relieved when she wrapped her legs around his thighs. "You drive me nuts, Abby." Didn't she know how vulnerable she was?

He wanted her in his bed. Now. Naked and needy. He wanted that more than anything in the whole world.

Abby patted his cheek and kissed his forehead. "We have to go inside. Remember? Your family?"

"Hell." She was right. "Tell me you brought an overnight bag."

"That wasn't part of the invitation."

"Abby…" He was at the end of whatever stores of patience he had accumulated.

She slid down his body and stepped away, gathering her sweater and smoothing her hair again. "I did," she said quietly. "But I'm not sure why."

"Don't lie to me, Abs. Or to yourself. We may not be a match made in heaven, but between the sheets we're dynamite."

He took her by the hand and dragged her inside. They found his family gathered in the room where Abby had interviewed Carter earlier that week.

The four adults were seated around a card table playing a game. Denise and Ernie had apparently decided to linger, given the drama that had transpired. The baby snoozed on a pallet on the floor.

Denise was the first to notice them. "There you are," she said, smiling. "Would you like us to deal you in?"

Carter managed not to cringe, though he could think of nothing more dreadful. "No, thanks," he said, his tone mild. "You guys finish your game. Abby and I will hang out. Or maybe have more dessert."

Cynthia Crane stood and approached them with a contrite expression on her face. "I'm sorry you overheard our conversation, dear."

Abby didn't smile. "But you're not sorry you questioned my presence here tonight."

Wow. Carter wanted to high-five somebody. Abby Carmichael had just put his mother in her place.

The older woman narrowed her eyes. "I love my son. It's normal for a mother to want the best for her children. That said, Carter is free to invite whomever he likes to his home. I'm glad I met you, Abby. You are a very interesting woman."

There was a collective exhale in the room when Cynthia returned to the game and left Carter and Abby to entertain themselves.

Half an hour later, the house was finally quiet. Carter shot Abby a wry glance. "Now you see why we built the guest cottage."

"I do," Abby said. But her laugh sounded forced.

"You okay?" He lifted her chin with a finger, looking deep into those dark brown eyes surrounded by thick inky lashes.

Abby stepped away, breaking the small contact. "I'm fine, Carter. Really. But I think I'll head back to town. Your family wants to spend time with you. It feels weird to be sneaking around."

"We're not *sneaking*," he protested. "We're two grown adults. I want you to stay the night." Her reluctance dented his mood.

She flipped her hair over her shoulder, unwittingly drawing his attention to the spot where her throat met her collarbone, a spot he would like to nibble. Soon.

"They'll be coming over for breakfast, right?"

"Not if I tell Denise to keep them away."

"Oh, Carter. This is complicated. I don't want to get in the way of you enjoying your family. You told me they don't visit all that often."

He shoved his hands in his pockets and leaned

against the door frame. "If you don't want to stay, just say so."

"I *do* want to stay." She played with her earring, pacing the confines of his living room. "But I don't want *them* to know I stayed."

"Well, that's easy. I'll set an alarm for seven. You can be on your way, and I'll pretend I slept alone. Although it's really nobody's damn business."

Humor lit her face. "As weird as this evening was, I do like your family."

He ducked and looked over his shoulder.

She frowned. "What are you doing?"

"Waiting for the lightning to strike. That's usually what I do when somebody tells a whopper. You can't honestly say you *like* my mother."

She scrunched up her face. "Maybe *like* is the wrong word. But she brought you into this world, so she can't be all bad."

His shoulders loosened, and he crossed the room to take her hands in his. "I've been wanting to get you out of this dress for hours. Swim first? Or straight to the main event?"

Abby realized that the window for changing her mind was over. Actually, as soon as she admitted she had an overnight case in her car, the course of the evening was set. Carter wanted her here, and she wanted to be here. In the end, nothing else mattered.

She snuggled up to his chest, sliding her arms around his waist. "We can swim later. Isn't there a full moon tonight? For now, I'm more than happy to see your bedroom again."

Abby realized a couple of things in the next hour. First, Carter was far less serious than the face he showed to the world. Beneath that mantle of responsibility was a man who liked to play.

And second, he knew way too much about how to pleasure a woman. The man made an art form out of removing her dress. He did it so slowly and with so much sensual heat, she was ready to dissolve into a puddle of lust by the time he had stripped her down to her panties.

They took a quick shower together, one that involved lots of soap and teasing. Then they dried off and returned to the bedroom.

Abby was less self-conscious now, more willing to let her gaze linger on Carter's aroused sex. He was a stud. No question. A very masculine man with the body of someone who did physical labor. If she were a sculptor, she would carve him, every sinew and muscle.

He scooped her up in his arms and nuzzled his nose against hers. "You cold?"

Her heart beat faster. "Not at all. Make love to me, Carter."

His face flushed with heat. "Whatever the lady wants."

For a split second, she wished she had used a different phrase. There was no love between them. How *could* there be? She didn't believe in love at first sight, and besides, these feelings she had were physical, not emotional. Carter made her body sing.

He didn't give her time for second-guessing. Soon,

he worshipped her, kissing from earlobes and eyelids to the throbbing spot at her center, making her squirm. She was close to coming already. She'd been aching for him since that moment when she had slipped out of this bed like a thief in the night.

"Now..." she begged.

He left her for mere seconds to take care of protection and came back to shift her thighs apart and thrust deep. The noise he made was half groan, half curse.

She understood what he didn't say. This was beyond words. He filled her completely, his hard sex claiming everything she offered willingly. Their joining was something more than the two of them slaking a sexual thirst. Rather, it was the kind of chemical reaction that fizzed and sparked and boiled over.

Because it was hot and urgent and not to be denied, Abby was swept up in a wave of sheer bliss. How insanely wonderful could a moment be? How *perfect*...

Carter surrounded her, aroused her and, paradoxically, protected her.

When her orgasm yanked her up and threw her into the abyss, she felt limp with joy, sated with pleasure.

In the aftermath, he pulled her against his side. She stretched one leg across his thighs and pillowed her cheek on his chest.

Abby wasn't asleep, and she wasn't 100 percent awake. She floated, wallowing in the seductive feeling of invincibility.

Carter played with her hair, his breath warm on the top of her head. "I can't feel my legs," he complained.

She pinched his upper thigh, hard enough to bruise. "I can."

"Brat."

"Bossy, arrogant rancher."

His raspy chuckle made her feel happy and warm. In Carter's embrace, she felt like herself. With the few other men she had let into her life on a sexual basis, she had always held something back, wary of being judged.

In this bed, with this man, her world was complete.

And that was scary as hell.

Finally, she lifted up on one elbow and smiled at him. "I'm not sleepy. Can we take a glass of wine out by the pool and enjoy the moonlight?"

His gaze was hooded, his hair mussed. "Of course, beautiful. But don't get dressed. We might take a dip. There's no one around to peek."

He gave her a robe out of his closet, a hotel-style garment that was soft and plush and smelled faintly of Carter's aftershave. For himself, he grabbed a towel and tucked it around his waist.

In the kitchen, he didn't bother with the overhead light as he gathered glasses and a corkscrew. Abby was glad. These minutes felt precious and private. She wanted to preserve this bubble of intimacy, to savor every moment of it.

Outside, the moon shone down serenely, illuminating the pool and chasing away shadows. They settled onto cushioned lounge chairs. Carter opened the wine and poured. When he clinked his glass against hers, he smiled. "To new friends. And beautiful cinematographers. I'm glad you stayed."

Abby wanted to say something nice in return, but her throat was tight, and her thoughts were all jumbled. Instead, she sipped her wine and wiggled her toes, feeling the peace of the summer night wash over her.

Beside her, Carter resembled a large, lazy jungle cat. His body was completely relaxed. So much so that it took her by surprise when he spoke.

"I want to see you again, Abby."

He laid it out there. No games.

"Your family is here all week, right?"

"Yes," he said. "But they don't bite."

"I'm not your girlfriend, Carter. It would be different if I were. You need to spend quality time with them. Besides, I have several more interviews lined up this week. I'll be busy."

Turning toward her, he pinned her with his blue gaze. "The weekend, then?"

"I'm flying out to LA on Friday. My father is going to help me begin to piece together my story. He's great at editing."

"When will you be back?" he asked.

"Midweek probably," she replied. "I'm bringing some camping gear then. Since there isn't any public lodging on Appaloosa Island, I have to find a way to spend the night and get those magical early morning shots. Camping is the best solution. If I can get permission."

"And after that?"

"I'll probably go home to New York, regroup and come back to Royal right before the festival starts."

"I see." He paused. "It sounds like you consider New York home, and not California. Is that true?"

"Yes. My mother wanted my school years to be uninterrupted. But summers and holidays were a roll of the dice." Abby raised the wineglass to her lips and took a sip. "Neither she nor my father meant to make me feel bad, but there was always an unspoken tug-of-war. I think that's when travel started to appeal to me. I could go where I wanted, when I wanted, without having to answer to anyone."

"Makes sense."

"I haven't told you much about my parents," she said quietly. "They still care about each other, even after all these years apart."

"Why did they split in the first place?" he asked curiously.

"Because their lives were too different. Once they got past the wild rush of falling in love and having me, the reality of day-to-day life didn't work." She shrugged. "My mom couldn't conceive of leaving New York. But my dad dreamed of becoming a filmmaker and needed the flexibility to go where the opportunities arose. Having a wife and a little baby held him back. Ultimately, my mother set him free to be who he was meant to be. And she found happiness and fulfillment on her own."

"Is this the part where I'm supposed to see the parallels? If so, I'm not convinced." A muscle ticked in his jaw. "I don't give a damn about the future right now. But I want to be with you, Abby."

The lump in her throat grew painfully. "I want to be with you, too."

A light breeze danced around them, ruffling the water, diluting the moon's reflection. The wine bottle was empty now. Abby felt mellow, but melancholy.

When Carter said nothing for long minutes, she blurted out the truth that had struck her tonight. "I envy you, you know."

He set his glass on the table. "How so?"

"Your family. I love my mom and dad, and they love me, but I've never had the kind of family unit the Cranes have. Even your brother-in-law is an integral part of that tight circle. I can tell that each of you would do anything for the others."

"Like taking over a huge ranch far too young?" Carter sighed. "I'm handling things now, though the first few years were tough. I grew up here, but suddenly sitting in the owner's seat was terrifying."

"Your father is proud of you."

"I hope so."

Abby was drenched in sadness suddenly. To come close to something so perfect and yet know it was out of reach shredded her emotions.

"I think I'll swim now," she said.

Eleven

Carter stayed where he was, his hands fisted on his thighs. Watching Abby shed his robe and dive gracefully into the water was an experience he couldn't describe. Her beauty in the moonlight made his heart ache.

When she surfaced, laughing, he felt something crack inside his chest, some wall of self-protection that had begun to crumble without his knowledge. Since Madeline's defection, he had put his emotions on hold, denying his needs, focusing on the ranch.

Tonight, beneath a full moon, sated sexually and slightly drunk on a bottle of very good wine, he felt reborn. Yet, at the same time, he knew nothing for certain.

Was he feeling lust and gratitude, or something more?

Abby swam and played like a creature familiar with the sea. He supposed she really was. With one home base in Malibu, she must have spent long hours on the beach, or frolicking in the Pacific.

Carter was jealous suddenly of every teenage boy and young man who had lain at her side, flirted with her, wallowed on a sandy blanket and kissed those perfect lips.

His breath sawed in and out of his lungs as if he was running full tilt. His heart pounded. He didn't know what to do. That very uncertainty was so novel, he was stunned.

At thirty-four, the world was his oyster. He had money and power and unlimited opportunity.

What he didn't have was a mate, a lover, a life partner.

With Madeline, he had seen her as he wanted her to be. His blindness had cost him greatly in terms of his pride and his confidence. Thankfully, he had ultimately realized that while she had treated him shabbily, she hadn't broken his heart.

He didn't want to make another impulsive mistake. Especially with so little time. He and Abby weren't ships passing in the night. They were high-speed trains on opposite tracks. This moment with her was nothing more than a blip.

She came to the side of the pool and waved at him. "Come join me."

He noticed that she was careful not to expose her naked breasts. The show of modesty amused him. "How's the water?"

"Somewhere between chilly and almost perfect."

"You'd better not be kidding." He dropped his towel and walked down the steps into the shallow end.

Abby stayed near the rope that marked deeper water. "It's your pool. You should know by now. Or do you never go skinny-dipping when you're alone?"

He strode through the water, stalking her, grinning when she ran out of her depth. "Stay put, little mermaid. Don't be scared."

She lifted her chin. "I'm not scared of you. But I'm not accustomed to being stark naked in public."

He glanced around the pool. "It's just us, Abs."

Finally, he was within touching distance—close enough to see the droplets of water beading on her arms, each one reflecting a tiny moon. Her dark hair floated around her, partially obscuring her bare breasts.

Was that intentional?

"Do you know how beautiful you are?" he whispered hoarsely.

She didn't respond. But a blink of her eyes could have meant anything.

He shook his head slowly. "I know you're smart and competent and career focused, and all those things strong women aspire to be. But damn, Abby, you're also incredibly lovely. The kind of lovely that makes a man wish he could paint you exactly the way you look right now."

"You're embarrassing me," she whispered.

"Oh? Does that mean you want me to stop talking?"

She nodded slowly. Even with the moon, he couldn't read the secrets hidden in her dark eyes. Carefully, he took a piece of her hair and tugged. She came to him willingly, her smile striking him dead in the chest, stealing his breath.

When their bodies met, they groaned in unison. Naked flesh to naked flesh. The water made them buoyant. He coaxed her legs around his waist.

"I like your…pool," she said, with a naughty grin.

He fondled her butt, feeling his sex flex and stir. "I like the way you're all wet and slick. Like a sea otter."

Her head fell back, and she laughed so hard one breast popped up above the water. "That's awful, Carter. No wonder you don't have a girlfriend."

He took them a few steps closer to the side of the pool. Then he kissed her long and slow. "If you're auditioning for the part, it's going really well," he muttered.

She clung to his shoulders as her smile dimmed. "I'm not an actress," she said. "What you see is what you get. Just a girl who's a friend."

The moon dipped behind a cloud, plunging them into darkness. "I want you again, Abby. Now."

"We can't, Carter. It's too dangerous."

Beneath the water he stroked her sex, entering her with two fingers. "Did I ever tell you I was a Boy Scout years ago? Always prepared?"

He leaned toward the side of the pool briefly and reached for the robe she had discarded, finding what he wanted.

Abby stared at him, mouth agape. "You hid a condom in my pocket? That's sneaky, Mr. Crane."

"Sneaky? Or very, very smart?"

He set her on her feet and tugged her by the hand. "Come toward the steps for a minute."

When he ripped open the packet and dealt with the latex, Abby watched. He liked that. A *lot*. Men had a tendency to show off for the opposite sex. He was no different.

He took her hand. "I'm ready. Are you?"

She ran her hand down his chest, stopping to toy with his navel. "I was born ready, cowboy."

They moved into deeper water. Carter scooped his hands under her hair and cupped her neck. "I'm glad you stopped to film the sunset that first night. Otherwise, we might never have met."

Now that she couldn't touch bottom, she clung to his shoulders. "I'll tell you a secret. The sunset was gorgeous, but I was filming *you*. Riding flat out. Horse and man moving as one. It was poetry in motion. I liked what I saw."

He kissed her slowly, intimately. "And now?"

"I'm super glad you dumped that skank Madeline."

This time he was the one to laugh uproariously. "Hell, Abby. If I'd been *married* to her, I'd probably have dumped her for you."

Abby smiled softly, running her thumb over his lower lip. "No," she said. "If you'd been married, you never would have looked at another female. I've learned a lot about you since I've come to Royal. You're a man of honor. A gentleman. The kind of guy all women want. But when they don't find him, they settle for less."

"You're buttering me up, Abs. I'm as flawed as anyone. For instance, right now I'd like to beg you to forget about your documentary and stay with me for a while."

She rested her head on his shoulder, her legs tangling with his. "It sounds like fun. But I know you're not serious, not really. We both see the bigger picture. Sometimes doing the sensible, mature thing sucks."

"Yeah," he said gruffly. "It does." He was done with talking. Nothing Abby had to say made him feel any better about their situation. His erection hadn't flagged, not even in the midst of a semiserious moment. In fact, holding her like this was pure torture. The moonlight. The silky water. The way Abby's body felt against his… His sex throbbed with urgency, even as his brain tried to draw out the pleasure.

Abby kissed his chin. "Take me, Carter. I want you so much I'm shaking."

It was true. He could feel the tremors in her body, could hear her fractured breathing. "Hang on, sweetheart."

He lifted her, aided by the water, and positioned her to slide down onto his swollen sex. The muscles in his arms quivered as he supported her weight. When they were joined, male to female, yin to yang, he cursed. "Damn, woman. You're killing me."

His knees were embarrassingly weak. Abby's body accepted his as if they had been designed for this exact joining. Her sex took him in and wrapped him tightly in blissful heat. The sensation was one he couldn't have imagined.

"I've never done this in the water," he said, the words breathless.

Abby pulled back so she could see his face. "Really?"

"Really."

He wasn't sure she believed him, but he was beyond

talking. He'd gone into this without overthinking the logistics. Now his body was driving him to seal the deal. "Abs?"

"Hmm?" She pressed kisses along his jawline.

"I need the wall."

Her lips curved. "I can handle that."

He lurched toward the metal stairs and gently pressed Abby to the right of them against the slightly rough surface of pool. The water was up to her chin. "Does this hurt?" He thrust into her while he asked the question, obviously not under control.

"I'm good," she said.

It was weird, weirder than he had anticipated. The water made his movements clumsy. Carter drove into her once, shifted, and then went deep again. He was close to coming, but what about the mermaid in his arms?

She had one hand wrapped around the metal steps. Her breasts pillowed against his chest. Leaning back, he reached between their bodies and found her most sensitive spot. As he thumbed it, Abby climaxed, a little cry echoing on the breeze.

Her inner contractions were all it took to set him off. He moaned and came hard. The pleasure was mind-blowing, yet at the same time, he found himself mentally cursing the way the water made it difficult to move like he wanted to…

Abby was limp in his embrace. He peeled her fingers from the step railing and put her hands behind his neck. "It looks more romantic in the movies, doesn't it?"

She rested her cheek against him. "I've got no complaints. Except that my fingers are getting pruney."

"Well, we can't have that."

With no small amount of regret, he separated their bodies. "Time to get out."

Abby refused to go first, so he dragged himself up the steps, dealt with the condom and reached down to take her hand. "Up you come."

It felt strange to be on firm ground. The night air seemed colder suddenly. Abby's arms were covered in gooseflesh. He fetched her a towel and grabbed the one on the lounger for himself.

She didn't say anything. Neither did he.

They walked back inside the house and down the hall to his room. "Do you want to shower again?" he asked, trying to be the gentleman she proclaimed him to be.

Abby yawned. "Nope. I just want to sleep."

They tumbled beneath the covers. He twined his arms and legs with hers and turned out the light.

His lover was asleep in seconds, her damp hair spread across his pillow.

Carter was not so lucky. He lay awake, staring into the darkness. An odd memory floated across his brain. Something from when he was six or seven years old. He'd heard a tale about a pearl that was so valuable, a man sold everything he had to purchase it.

At the time, he'd thought it was a stupid story. His Sunday school teacher had been a stern, no-nonsense woman who—as Carter remembered it—had little patience for wiggly boys who only wanted to be let loose outside.

He turned his head and watched Abby sleep. Unable to resist, he kissed her forehead and gently stroked her hair. Even if the merchant's actions made more sense now, Carter couldn't follow suit. The ranch belonged to him on paper, but its legacy was a joint venture, a family bond.

Even worse, he couldn't repeat the mistakes he made with Madeline. He'd met her at that damned wedding and proposed to her far too soon, without even knowing her. His impulsive behavior had doomed the relationship from the start.

But Abby was different, wasn't she? There was no artifice in her, no selfishness. And Carter was older and wiser.

The more he thought about his situation, the more trapped he felt. In that moment, he felt the sting of loss.

Abby was right there beside him, but he knew their time was short.

Sometimes life was a bitch.

Abby didn't leave a note this time. They had come too far for that. She'd set her alarm for six thirty. When it buzzed, she silenced it quickly. Carter never moved.

After she showered and dressed, she sat down on the bed at his hip. "Carter," she whispered.

He grunted and rolled onto his back, scrubbing his hands over his face. "What time is it?"

"Barely seven. I wanted to say goodbye before I left."

He sat up and frowned. "What's the rush?"

"We talked about this," she said quietly. "Your family will be over for breakfast soon. I'm heading back to the hotel."

"And did we agree on anything for when you return?"

Her smile cost her. Leaving Carter like this was a physical pain in her chest. If she'd had her wish, she would have lingered to play all day. "I'll let you know when I get back from New York." She leaned down to kiss him. The cheek seemed too casual for what they had shared. But the mouth was dangerous.

She chose the mouth anyway, her lips melding with his. Carter was warm. His big arms wrapped around her and held her close.

He nuzzled her forehead with his. "You sure you don't want to stay a few more minutes?"

"No. It wouldn't be a few minutes, and you know it. Tell your family I enjoyed meeting them. Bye, Carter."

She fled the house, perilously close to letting him sweet-talk her into staying. But she knew what was right. Family was important.

Every moment of the week that followed, she worked herself hard, researching, filming, interviewing. She had thought that she and Carter might text back and forth casually. But neither of them initiated a virtual conversation. After all, what was there to say?

She missed him terribly.

Though her personal life was a mess, her professional life flourished. Most notably, Lila arranged for Abby to have access to the Texas Cattleman's Club to shoot interior montages after hours. With patrons on-site, the permissions involved would have been too complicated.

Abby began working on a voice-over script that would narrate this particular section, touching on the history, but also pointing out how the club was central to life in Royal even in the twenty-first century.

Carter was a member. No surprise there.

When Abby had first sat in on the meeting of the advisory board, she had seen part of the club, of course. Now, with no one in residence but the night watchman, she was free to roam the halls and peek into the various rooms.

She was surprised to see a state-of-the-art day care on the premises. The center was a bright, cheerful place with murals on the walls and everything a young child could possibly want.

Lila had given her a roster of current members and oddly, Billy Holmes was included. He'd only lived in Royal a few years, and he didn't own a ranch. But other people of influence in the community were recognized for their accomplishments, so maybe Billy had been inducted based on merits Abby wasn't privy to during her short visit with him.

The night watchman himself had related how an F4 tornado a few years before had destroyed part of the town and even damaged this fine old building. The community had pulled together to rebuild Royal stronger and better than before.

At last, Abby had all the footage she needed, in truth, far more than she would ever be able to use. But she was fascinated by what seemed like a vestige of the Old

West. Money talked. Here in Royal, it talked louder in this building than almost anywhere else.

When she packed up her gear and wandered back to the front lobby, she found the night watchman talking to someone familiar. Carter.

Her pulse jumped. She approached the two men calmly. "What brings you here, Carter? I thought I was the only after-hours visitor."

They made their goodbyes to the guard and stepped outside. Carter took two of her bags and carried them to the car. "I wanted to see you before you left," he said.

"Oh." She didn't know how to respond to that. "Is your family still in town?"

"They're leaving in the morning, too. Maybe you'll see them at the airport."

I hope not, she thought wryly. "Did you have a good visit?"

"Actually, yes. It was great. My brother-in-law helped me around the ranch. Dad's health is doing well, so he joined us occasionally. It was especially fun to spend time with the baby. She's changing every day."

"And your mom and sister?"

"My mother was extremely well-behaved. I think she feels guilty about what happened with you. My sister, on the other hand, told me not to let you get away."

Abby winced. "But you told her we weren't a thing?"

He shoved his hands in his pockets and leaned against the car. "I did."

"Good."

Her stomach curled with regret. She had always

hated goodbyes. "I should go," she said softly. "Thanks for stopping by."

"I was hoping you might invite me up to your room."

And there it was again. The insidious temptation that made a mockery of all her grown-up plans.

What could it hurt, the devil on her shoulder whispered.

He'll break your heart, said her conscience.

Five seconds passed. Then ten. "I have a very early flight, Carter. And I haven't finished packing. I'm sorry."

He didn't react visibly to her polite refusal, but he straightened and took her hand, reeling her in with ease, since she had no intention of protesting.

His mouth settled on hers, his lips firm and masculine. She breathed in his scent, trying to memorize it. He tasted of cinnamon and coffee.

"Don't forget about me, Abs, while you're gone," he muttered. "I'll miss you."

Her eyes stung with tears. "I'll miss you, too."

He kissed her again. This one almost took her down. It wasn't him she was resisting; it was her own yearning. At last, he let her go. "Keep in touch, Abby. I want to know how you're doing."

"I will," she promised.

He opened her car doors, put her gear in the back seat and then leaned down to watch her fasten her seat belt as he closed her in. "Do you need a ride to the airport?"

"No, thanks. I'll be turning in the rental car."

"Ah, yes."

Her window was lowered, letting out the heat that

accumulated even at this hour. He had a hand on the sill. She put her fingers over his. "Bye, Carter. Thanks for everything."

Then she put the car in gear and drove away, looking in the rearview mirror only once to see him standing tall and alone in the club parking lot.

Twelve

Abby's father met her at the airport. He was a tall, barrel-chested Black man with kind eyes and a gentle sense of humor. Though they had lived on opposite coasts for most of her life, she had always known that he would drop everything and come to her if she ever needed him.

Her dad negotiated the horrible traffic without flinching. He truly was a Californian after all these years. They stopped at Abby's favorite seafood restaurant before heading on to the house. Over lunch, she brought up a subject that had been occupying her mind recently.

"Daddy, when you and Mom first separated, did you know you were doing the right thing?"

He seemed surprised, but he answered readily

enough. "Yes. We both did. The hard part was how much I adored you. We wanted to stay together for your sake, but we knew it couldn't work. Sometimes people come into our lives for a season, Abby. Your mother and I were very happy for a time, but life shifted us onto different paths."

"I understand." She didn't. Not really. It was hard for her to imagine loving someone and then *not* loving them.

That was the last of the personal conversation, even during the drive to the coast. She sensed the introspection made him uncomfortable. After she was settled into her old bedroom, they met out on the back veranda overlooking the Pacific. Her father had done very well in his career. His neighbors up and down this stretch of Malibu were actors and producers and other luminaries.

Though the land had increased in value over the years, her father's house was relatively modest. He had no interest in redecorating or following fashion trends. Right now, Abby was grateful. It was comforting to know that some things stayed the same.

They watched the sun go down.

She worked up her courage and took the plunge. "Daddy?"

"Hmm?"

"What would you think if Mom and I came out for Labor Day and stayed with you? Just the three of us."

He'd been watching the water; now he turned to face her. "I have no problem with that, baby girl. I've always told you that your mother is welcome here. Is something going on with you?"

"No. Not really. I just thought it would be nice for the three of us to get together. Now that I'm an adult, too."

"It will depend on your mother," he said with a wistful smile. "You know how stubborn she is. I'm sure she'd rather do a get-together like that on her turf."

"True. Well, I'll ask her, and let you know."

Afterward, her father excused himself to go make a work-related phone call. His state-of-the-art studio was upstairs. For the next couple of days, she knew that the two of them would bond over her fledgling movie.

For now, she lingered to enjoy the stars and the sultry ocean breeze.

What was Carter doing tonight? She regretted not letting him stay with her the evening before, but it would only have made things harder. He was wrapping himself around her heartstrings without even trying.

Her father rarely asked about her personal life. Maybe because he didn't want any questions in return. They loved each other, but certain lines were never crossed.

In many ways, her relationship with her mother was the same. Abby loved her parents and had always known that she was loved unconditionally in return. But her family was different than Carter's. *Very* different.

However, as much as Abby had yearned for a "normal" family while growing up, she knew how lucky she was.

The long weekend passed in a blur. Her father had a keen eye for visual storytelling. Though he was always quick to point out that it was her project, *her baby*, the suggestions he made for her documentary were spot-on.

By the time he put her on a plane for New York, she was ecstatic at how the film was coming together. And more confident, too. If this project turned out as well as she was expecting it to, she would be on her way to a promising career.

She was already almost regretting the flight to New York. It wouldn't have been a big deal to simply fly from LA to Royal. Still, even though this would be a super short visit, she wanted to swap out some of her clothes, and she also hoped to talk to her mother about Carter. If the right moment arose.

Her flight landed on time Monday afternoon. Abby took a cab from LaGuardia to Manhattan. She and her mother lived in a high rise on a quiet block of East 77th Street. Abby had never questioned her mother's finances. There was money from Abby's grandparents. And she was certain her father had paid child support. Beyond that, she only knew that she and her mother lived a very comfortable life.

When she took the elevator to the tenth floor and unlocked the door, her mother wasn't home. No real surprise. But for the first time, the apartment's quiet emptiness struck her as a little sad.

What would it be like when Abby moved out for good? Did her mother have any desire for grandchildren? Some women didn't.

Abby did some laundry and rifled through her closet to repack her suitcase. On a whim, she folded a beautiful, fire-engine red evening dress and added it to the pile. Lila had mentioned the possibility of some special events surrounding the festival kickoff. Abby wanted to be ready.

It was hard to admit that in the back of her mind, she was already picturing herself wearing that sexy dress for Carter. Days ago, he had asked her to stay in touch. But she hadn't known what to say. When he didn't text either during their time apart, she had assumed he was busy or distracted or both.

Or maybe he had decided a clean break was the best.

Abby picked up her phone and stared at the screen. She had lots of emails and texts, but not the one she so desperately wanted.

Her fingers had a mind of their own. Quickly, she composed a message before she could change her mind.

Hey, Carter… I'm in New York now. My dad was super helpful with my film. We enjoyed catching up. Hope things are good at Sunset Acres…

It was a breezy, nonpersonal text. She almost deleted it, but then she sucked in a breath and hit Send.

Now that she was far away from Royal, it seemed almost ludicrous that she had indulged in an exhilarating, short-lived affair with a sexy, rugged Texan. The list of things they *didn't* have in common was depressingly long.

Had he already forgotten about her? Had she been an easy mark to him?

It was painful to consider. She honestly thought he was as caught up in the magic as she was. But maybe she was kidding herself.

Her beautiful, stylish, blond-haired mother made it home at six and brought food from Abby's favorite Chinese restaurant. Both her parents spoiled her when she was around. It was nice, but despite being twenty-four years old, Abby was in that odd stage between being a college student and a fully grown adult.

In any other place in the country, she might already have her own apartment by now. New York's cost of living was exorbitant, though, and her mother had often said Abby was welcome to use this apartment as home base for as long as she needed it.

Over a combo meal of various chicken and rice dishes, Abby mentally rehearsed how she was going to present the Labor Day idea. Something about the prospect of having her mom and dad together in Malibu, with her, excited Abby. Was she re-creating a childhood fantasy? A time she barely remembered?

Her motives were murky.

Before she could make her pitch, her mother set down her glass of wine and gave Abby a nervous smile. "I'm glad you're here, sweetheart. I have something I need to tell you, and I didn't want to do it over the phone."

Abby was alarmed. "Are you sick?"

"Oh, no. Nothing like that." Her mother fiddled with her chopsticks. "The thing is… I've met someone. A nice man who works in the financial district. He came in to have a painting appraised, and we hit it off. He asked me out to dinner, and well…things snowballed. He's asked me to move in with him."

"Mom!" Abby gaped, her brain swirling. "How long ago was this?"

"Back in February. You've been traveling a lot, and I didn't want to say anything until I knew if it was going anywhere."

Abby was shocked to the core. She didn't remember her mother ever dating anyone, which now that she thought about it was highly unlikely. Maybe her mom had been discreet for Abby's sake. Or maybe she had put her personal life on hold until her daughter was old enough to fend for herself.

"I'm happy for you, Mom. Really."

Her mother beamed. "I'd love for you to meet him, but I suppose it will have to be when you're finished with that festival project. August, maybe?"

"I'd like that."

"And about this apartment…"

"You should sell it," Abby told her. "I'll find a place. Don't worry about me."

Her mother grimaced. "I'm not going to rush into marriage. I'd rather you keep the apartment for now. That way, if things don't work out for me, I won't end up looking for some place to live."

"Are you unsure about this relationship? Is that it?"

Her mother's face glowed. "Oh, no. Not at all. Bradley is a wonderful man. We have fun together. And we laugh a lot. But I failed at marriage once. It's made me gun-shy, I guess. For now, I just want to enjoy his company and see what happens."

Half a dozen emotions buffeted Abby. Time never stood still. Her parents had been divorced for almost two decades, but this new development felt like a threat.

That was dumb. After all, Abby wasn't a child anymore. Her mother deserved to be happy.

Clearly, there would be no mini family reunion in Malibu.

Her eyes burned. "Tell this Bradley person that he's found a jewel. I love you, Mom. This is wonderful news."

They both stood. Hugged tightly.

A few moments later, Abby put her dishes in the dishwasher and threw away the take-out cartons. "I need some exercise after sitting on a plane forever. You want to come with me? A walk in the park, maybe? It's too hot to run."

Her mother shook her head. "Thanks, sweetie. But I have some work to do, and Bradley will probably call in a bit. Will you be okay on your own?"

"Of course."

Abby changed clothes and went downstairs. Out on the pavement, the heat was oppressive. Instead of her usual three-mile run, she decided to walk the streets.

New York was *home*. She loved the hustle and bustle and even the crowds in Times Square. The city was huge and vibrant, and always *open*. Where else could you get a doughnut and coffee at 2:00 a.m.? Or a pizza.

The clothes shopping and the bookstores energized her. She found entertainment in the trendy boutiques and the high-end fashion empires that might not have what she wanted or needed, but were fun to explore anyway. Everything about the city of her birth was part of her DNA.

Yet, for the first time, she felt something was missing. Sex with Carter was great, but she yearned to hear his laugh. To enjoy his droll sense of humor. Her day felt empty and flat without him.

What did that mean? Was she in too deep?

She lost track of how far she walked. Surrounded by strangers, she nevertheless felt completely at home. Alone, but not lonely.

When it was time to head back, she was no closer to making a decision. Truthfully, there was no decision to make. If she wanted to sleep with Carter Crane a few more times, she could do that. He'd be happy to oblige. She was sure of it.

Why did she have to get swept off her feet by a man who lived several hundred miles away? As much as she cared for him, why indulge in something that had no future?

It was a question with no answer. Or at least not one she wanted to hear.

Even worse, Carter had never responded to her text. What did that mean? Was he done with her?

Tuesday flew by. Abby had lunch with a couple of friends. They had known each other since the beginning of high school and always managed to pick up right where they left off. Abby wanted to tell them about Carter, but she felt self-conscious. She wasn't in a relationship with him. Just because he had seen her naked, and she was crazy about him didn't mean anything was going to come of it. Carter was Carter, and Abby was Abby.

They were great in bed, but morning always came.

After lunch, she stopped in at a high-end outdoor

adventure store and picked out a small tent and the most basic of camping supplies. Her family had never done the camping thing, but Abby was certain she could make it through one night in the relative wilds of Appaloosa Island. Shooting at dawn was one of her passions. The morning light made cinema magic.

She plunked down her credit card and paid an ouch-worthy premium for two-day delivery to Texas. As the day passed, she grew more anxious about returning to Royal. Would Carter expect to see her again? And could *she* handle seeing him again now that she was at least being honest with herself about her feelings?

Abby and her mother went out for dinner that evening. They even dressed up and made a celebration of it. The meal was fun and delicious and just like old times.

But the world was turning, and life was changing. Abby had to change along with it whether she wanted to or not.

Wednesday morning, her mother gave her a tight hug before heading off to work. "We'll make a date for August," she said. "Whenever you know your plans and your schedule for coming home. I'm glad the documentary is going so well."

"Thanks, Mama." Abby hugged her again. "Bradley had better treat you right, or he'll have to answer to me."

Her mother laughed, her face alight with happiness. "I'll be sure to tell him."

After the door closed, Abby had half an hour to kill before her rideshare arrived. She stood at the living room window and looked beyond the nearest buildings to the slice of Central Park she could see.

It would be hard to find a view more different from the one in her memories of Royal, Texas.

She wasn't a weepy woman, but she felt alarmingly emotional. What had happened to her? Why was she drawn back to a Texas town with red dirt and no subway system? Lots of cows, but no Broadway.

The ostensible reason was her project about Soiree on the Bay. That much was true. But she wouldn't lie, even to herself. Her documentary had made room on the shelf for something, or someone, equally important. Carter Crane. Abby's feelings for him went far beyond the physical.

How could she be falling for a man who was so wrong for her?

At the airport, she boarded the jet, unable to ignore the undercurrent of excitement she felt. By dinnertime, she would be back on Carter's home turf. The hotel had even blocked the same room she had been in last week. Lila's recent text said everything was a go for the overnight campout on Appaloosa Island.

The festival dates were fast approaching. Abby had a lot to accomplish before then. Even if she wanted to, she couldn't afford to fool around with Carter all the time. She had to focus on her task.

Unfortunately, today's flight itinerary had two different connections, first Atlanta, then Dallas. By the time the plane finally landed in Royal, it was almost dinnertime.

Abby felt let down when there was no one at the airport to greet her. Which made no sense at all, because she hadn't told anyone her plans. Had she actually been hoping for a big, romantic scene where Carter met her at baggage claim and swore they could juggle all their differences?

She snorted inwardly as she waited for her luggage. There was a reason she produced documentaries instead of rom-coms. Her subjects were framed in truth, not romantic fiction. *She* controlled the outcome, not the notoriously capricious whims of fate.

By the time she made it to the hotel, her stomach grumbled loudly. She checked in, threw her things in the room, brushed her teeth, fluffed her hair and then headed out again. She didn't want room service, and she didn't want to eat in the hotel dining room alone. Not tonight.

Fortunately, there was a great pizza place down the street.

The elevator moved far too slowly. Or maybe Abby's patience was shot. That was the trouble with air travel. It took all day to make a little progress.

When she stepped into the beautifully appointed hotel lobby, the first person she saw was Carter. He was leaning against a column, dressed in dark slacks and wearing a snow-white dress shirt with the sleeves rolled up and cowboy boots.

His slow smile took the starch out of her knees.

He straightened and met her halfway. "Hey, Abs. I missed you."

And then he caught her up in his arms and kissed her so long and so hard that the clerk at the front desk clapped and cheered, as did a couple of guests.

Abby's face was on fire when she pulled away. "I missed you, too," she whispered.

"Where were you headed?"

"Dinner. I've been on planes all day, and little packets of peanuts don't cut it. I need real food."

"How 'bout I take you to one of my favorite hole-in-the-wall places? It's quirky, but the food is fantastic."

She looked into his blue eyes, seeing the genuine pleasure reflected there. His enthusiasm made her feel good. After two somewhat odd visits with her parents, she'd been adrift. Unsettled. Carter's presence was exactly what she needed.

As he helped her into his car, she sat back and sighed, feeling her bad mood and her gloomy outlook improve. The Caballero Cantina was just as Carter had described. The rough plaster walls inside were yellow and orange and decorated with colorful murals.

The hostess gave Carter a smile that was too flirty for Abby's peace of mind, but the young woman seated them at a nice table in a corner shielded from view by the high back of an adjacent booth.

Abby's mouth watered as she perused the Tex-Mex menu. At Carter's recommendation, she ordered a fajita bowl. While they waited, she ate far too many chips and queso. But hey—what was the point of visiting Texas and not indulging in the local cuisine? The meal, when it came, was incredible.

Carter laughed at her. "You like the food?"

"How come I've been here all this time, and you're just now telling me about this place?"

"I've been busy, I guess."

Her stomach clenched. "I'll admit, I was surprised to see you tonight."

"I thought we agreed to touch base when you returned."

She tilted her head and studied his bland expression, searching for any evidence that he was as calm as he looked. "Touch base? Or go all the way home?"

Carter leaned forward and wiped a tiny drip of cheese from her chin with his fingertip. His crooked smile was sexy and wicked. "I guess that's up to you."

Abby considered inviting him back to her hotel room, but something stopped her. She wanted him too much. Her feelings weren't so hard to decipher. She was falling in love with him, and she knew they were the least likely couple in Royal to make a go of things.

In a last-ditch nod to self-preservation, she forced herself to speak lightly. "I'm sure there will be some base touching. But I'm exhausted, Carter. Rain check? Please?"

His smile faded as his gaze narrowed. "Are you okay, Abs? What happened while you were gone?"

"Nothing really." Oh, heck. She might as well tell him. "I found out that my mother has a boyfriend. And they're moving in together."

He sat back and whistled. "That must have been a shock."

"You could say that. I didn't even know she was dating."

"Will you still feel comfortable living with her?" he asked.

Trust Carter to cut through to the basics of a situation. "Actually, she's moving in with *Bradley*. She wants me to keep our apartment, so she'll have a place to go back to if things don't work out."

"That's pretty cynical."

She sighed. "You'd have to know my mother. She's a pragmatist through and through."

"Should I say, *I'm sorry, Abby*?"

"That's just it. I don't know how to feel. When I was with my dad, I was making a fun little plan for the three of us to hang out in Malibu for Labor Day weekend. He was okay with it. He and my mom are cordial. But I didn't know about *Bradley*."

"You're gonna have to stop saying his name like that," he cautioned.

"I know."

Carter leaned back in his chair and ate another chip. "I have news that might cheer you up."

Thirteen

"Oh? Tell me." Abby was instantly intrigued, especially because Carter's smile was teasing. As if he was eager to spring his surprise on her.

He took a long swig of his drink, drawing out the suspense. "You mentioned camping out to get some shots on Appaloosa Island with the morning light…"

"Yes."

"Well, I called in a favor. A couple of my college buddies went in together five or six years back and bought one of those fancy-ass houses at the western end of the island. They share it between the families. I checked, and this weekend no one is using it. If you want to, you and I can go out there and spend a night or two. It's very private. Luxurious. What do you think?"

She thought about the camping gear she'd had

shipped to the hotel. But when she balanced that against spending a romantic weekend with Carter, it was no contest. "I think it sounds great!" She knew what she was agreeing to, and why. This would be one last wonderful rendezvous with Carter. After this weekend, she had to go cold turkey.

"Good." He grinned. "I'll tell them we'd like to use the house."

"Should I offer to pay for it?"

"Nope. I'll send them each a case of their favorite whiskey, and they'll be good."

When the meal was over, Carter drove her back to the hotel. Already, she was second-guessing the fact that she had kept him at bay tonight. She had to get her head on straight. She wasn't really in love with him, was she?

The fact that she didn't know for sure made her jittery.

He pulled up under the hotel portico but didn't get out. "Sleep well, Abby."

She turned sideways in her seat. "Thank you for dinner. And thank you for working out the Appaloosa Island thing. That will be a whole lot better than sweating in a tent."

He ran a finger along her chin, his touch arousing her despite its innocence. "I'm hoping *I'll* get a chance to make you sweat, but that's up to you. We can hang out as friends. I don't expect sexual favors in exchange for our accommodations."

"I never thought you did." She reached across the console and kissed him softly on the lips. He went still but didn't react. "I want you, Carter, but I have a few things to figure out. Give me time."

"However long you need, Abs." He twined a strand of her hair around his finger. "I won't hurt you. I care about you, Abby."

The stark sincerity in his voice was exactly what she was afraid of... Carter *did* care about her. She knew that. And she felt the same way about him. But she didn't want to lose control of the situation. As long as she kept her expectations clear, everything would be okay.

She ignored those last five words he said, mostly because she didn't know how to respond.

The festival was fast approaching. After that, Abby would be spending a lot of time in LA working on the documentary. When the film was done, she would likely go back to New York. And meet *Bradley*.

"What time this weekend?" she asked.

"I'll pick you up Friday at six. We can eat a picnic in the car. Amanda Battle's diner offers that kind of thing."

"Sounds perfect. What do I need to bring?"

The uniformed hotel employee kept giving them glances, as if worried they were blocking the drive. This time it was Carter who leaned toward Abby. He put a large warm hand behind her neck and coaxed her closer for a blistering kiss that made her quiver. "The house is fully furnished," he said huskily. "All you need is a toothbrush and a swimsuit. But on second thought, maybe just the toothbrush."

When he laughed softly, Abby wanted to forget all about her rules. She wanted to drag him upstairs to her bed. Instead, she exhaled and opened her door. "Good night, Carter. Sweet dreams."

He got out of the car and rested one arm on top of the door to give her one last smoldering smile. "You, too, Abs. We can compare notes later."

And then he was gone.

The mirror on one wall of the elevator showed a woman who was weary from a long day of travel, yet also flushed with excitement. Carter did that to her. He made everything a little brighter, a little more vibrant.

That night as she showered and got ready for bed, she pondered the implications of spending the weekend with him. It was a work trip, sure. But with plenty of time for fun. She told herself this was as far as she would let things go.

They hadn't even known each other a month. Surely this sexual attraction would burn itself out soon. She was a novelty to him.

Furthermore, she could think of at least a dozen reasons why the two of them could never be a real couple.

Bottom line? As much as she liked him, and was maybe even falling for him, she was more like her mother than she realized. Carter wasn't part of the big picture. He wasn't Abby's *future*.

Carter went into town Thursday with a list of errands his ranch foreman would have been happy to tackle. But he was hoping to bump into Abby. How pathetic was that? He had resorted to acting like a middle school boy. All hormones and no sense.

He didn't see Abby at all, but he did run into Lila at

the post office. She was in line in front of him. They chatted briefly, but when he exited, she was waiting for him.

"May I speak to you for a minute, Carter?" she asked.

"Of course." They took advantage of a patch of shade beneath a large tree. "What's up?"

"It's Abby," she said. "I know it's not my business, but it sounds like the two of you are getting close."

He tensed. "Once again, Royal's grapevine is operating on all cylinders."

"Don't be mad. I'm just worried about her. She doesn't know many people here, at least not on a deeper level. And after Madeline, you haven't dated much."

"Is there a point to any of this?" he asked impatiently.

"Yes, there is." She looked him square in the eye. "What's the deal with Abby? You know she's not staying. And you know you won't leave."

His jaw tightened. "Abby and I are just having fun. And yes, it hasn't escaped me that she's too much like Madeline for any kind of long-term relationship. Abby is big-city dreams, and I'm a Royal rancher. It doesn't get much more different than that."

"She's young, Carter."

"Not that much younger than you."

"Maybe not. But beneath that big-city polish, I think she's vulnerable. You could hurt her. Why take the chance?"

"You and Zach are total opposites, too," Carter pointed out, trying not to reveal his frustration. "But you're making it work."

"Because Zach decided he wanted to stay in Royal," she said.

Lila was giving voice to every reservation Carter had about Abby. "I like her," he said slowly. "A lot. And I care about her well-being. More than I've cared about any woman in a long time. I know this thing between us is temporary. But I haven't made any promises, and neither has she. You'll have to trust me on this. Abby and I know what we're doing."

The distress on Lila's face was genuine. "I hope so, Carter. You're a good man. I know you wouldn't lie to her. But sometimes we want what we can't have."

"I'll be careful," he said. "You have nothing to worry about."

Carter carried Lila's words like a stone in his shoe for the rest of that day and into Friday. Should he call off the trip to Appaloosa Island? Let Abby go camping alone as she had originally planned? His idea about the house had seemed innocent enough, but now he didn't know. Was it wrong to take what Abby had to give, knowing it could never be anything more than this moment in time?

By the time he picked her up Friday at six, his gut was in knots. Most of that tension subsided when he saw her. The smile she gave him as she slid into the passenger seat was happy and carefree.

Lila was worrying over nothing.

Abby wasted no time digging into the wicker hamper. "I'm starving," she said. "Can you eat and drive at the same time?"

"Not a problem."

He headed out of town and onto the highway that would take them south to Mustang Point. Abby handed him a ham sandwich and opened a bag of chips. "Royal is getting really excited about the festival. People were talking about it everywhere I went today."

Carter snorted. "Wait until the shops are overrun with tourists and all the garbage cans are spilling over into the streets."

She opened a can of soda and shook her head slowly. "You really are a Scrooge, Carter Crane. New York has tons of people—tourists, too. But we get along very well."

"To each his own, I guess," he grumbled.

"Why don't we talk about something we can both agree on…books? Movies?"

The trip passed quickly. Abby seemed determined to put aside their differences. That was fine with Carter. He knew how very *unalike* they were. That was the problem.

Abby had read and reread the Harry Potter books, but also enjoyed political biographies. Carter was a Grisham fan and studied military history. They both agreed that the movie business was relying too much on blockbusters and not branching out enough.

When they finished their meal, Abby tucked the debris back in the hamper and returned it to the back seat. "I have a tiny bit of bad news," she said.

He shot her a sideways glance, seeing the apologetic look she gave him. "Oh?"

"I know you and I were planning to stay the whole weekend at your friends' house, but I got an invitation today for a black-tie reception at the Bellamy. It's a last-minute kickoff event on Saturday night for Soiree on the Bay, VIP only. They're going to hand out sample schedules, and I think one of the bands is going to play a few songs. I really need to be there."

"No problem," he said, refusing to admit he was disappointed. Having Abby naked and willing for an entire weekend had been a tantalizing prospect. "Am I invited?" he asked, tongue in cheek.

She took him seriously. "You probably are, but in any case, you're my plus-one…if you're willing."

He reached out and took her hand, lifting it to his mouth so he could kiss her fingers. "I know how important this documentary is to you. And I want to support you. So yes, I'd be happy to be your date."

"Great." Her grin was smug, as if she had talked him into something against his will. Little did she know that he would do almost anything to make her happy. It was a sobering realization for a man who walked through life alone.

He had never wanted to depend on a woman again. Yet here he was, twining his life with hers. What was that old saying? Give a man enough rope and he'll hang himself? Carter was heading for a calamity of some sort. A dramatic end-of-the-road thing. And probably sooner than later.

By the time they caught the ferry at Mustang Point, crossed the water and then drove to the inhabited western end of the island, the sun was low in the sky. He handed his phone to Abby. "Read me the directions from that text."

The instructions were simple enough. Soon, they were pulling into the driveway of what could only be described as a seafront villa. The architectural style was Italian.

Even Carter was impressed, and he was used to the immense wealth in Royal. This was over-the-top in every way.

Carter chuckled as they carried their things inside. "You pick a bedroom, Abs. Plenty to choose from."

He followed her down a hall. "This one," she said. "Look at the view."

One entire wall of the master suite was glass. Actually, there were three similar master suites, but this one was the closest to the pool.

They stood at the huge windows and used the binoculars they found on a nightstand. Dolphins gamboled fairly close to shore, probably fishing for their dinner. Sailboats streaked across the bay. Palm trees, planted by landscapers, added drama to the sunset scene.

Unselfconsciously, as if it were the most natural thing in the world, Abby rested her head on his shoulder. "What should we do first?" she asked.

His body tightened. What he *wanted* to say was crude and self-evident to any man with a pulse. But he could wait. Maybe.

"How about a swim? And then an early bedtime? Since you have to be up before dawn."

She laughed softly. "I hope *bedtime* is a euphemism for something."

"Hell, yeah…"

They changed clothes in different bathrooms. Abby

still occasionally exhibited a frustrating reticence around him. As if she were guarding some part of herself. Yet the more she held back, the more he wanted to push for more.

They met out at the pool. Abby was wearing a gold bikini that made his heart slug hard in his chest. Her long, toned legs, narrow waist and high, rounded breasts were showcased to perfection.

He cleared his throat. "Nice swimsuit, Abs."

She pulled her hair into a ponytail and secured it with an elastic band. "Thanks. I picked up a few more clothes when I was in New York. I honestly didn't know what I would need when I packed the first time."

He followed her down the shallow stairs into the pool, side by side. "What did you think Texas was going to be like?"

She shrugged as they waded deeper. "I didn't really know. Except for tales about everything being bigger in Texas." Without warning, she tweaked the front of his swim trunks. "That part turned out to be true." Laughing at his look of shock, she did a shallow dive and escaped to the deep end.

He chased her instinctively, energized by the game. But Abby was fast and nimble. Slippery, too. It was several minutes before he had her corralled against the side of the pool. He kissed her, tasting warm woman and anticipation. "You asked me to give you time, Abby. What did you mean by that? Time for what?"

"I couldn't decide what to do about you. About us."

"And now?" Her spiky eyelashes collected water droplets and let them fall, looking like tears.

Her smile was shaky. "I don't want to be serious right now. I'm like Cinderella at the ball. My time in Royal is running out. Let's have fun this weekend, Carter. That's all."

He should be happy. No-strings sex. With a beautiful woman who made him laugh. Why did her answer disturb him? "If that's what you want."

"It is," she said.

Abby curled her arms around Carter's neck and kissed him. Like every time before, the taste of him went straight to her head. Like hard liquor. She felt the strength in his gentle hold and sensed his frustration that was perhaps even more than physical. Neither of them liked the way this was playing out, but they were both trapped.

She loved the feel of his body against hers. The differences were stark and arousing. Carter was a man in his prime, his muscles the product of hard physical labor. She was rapidly becoming addicted to his flashing grin and twinkling blue eyes.

But was she really the kind of woman who would give up everything for a man?

He seemed fond of her. And yes, they were dynamite in bed. But if she even *considered* making such a huge change in her life, it would have to be for one reason only. Love.

She shuddered in his arms, relishing the way he commanded the kiss and changed it from playful and affectionate to intense and erotic. Their bodies recognized each other. Whether it was the novelty of being with someone new and different, or a deeper connection, she and Carter were made for each other when it came to sexual chemistry.

His heavy erection pulsed at her belly. "I want you," he rasped, his chest heaving against her breasts.

They hadn't been in the pool long at all. Abby didn't care. All she wanted was Carter. "Yes," she whispered back.

They took time to play in the outdoor shower, rinsing off the chlorine and stripping off their suits. There was no one to witness the moment when Carter scooped up a naked Abby in his arms and strode back to the house.

She knew suddenly that this precious moment was her swan song with Carter. The poignant knowledge was a knife to her heart, the pain searing her composure.

It took everything she had to conceal her turmoil.

In the bedroom, Carter abandoned her only long enough to grab towels from the bathroom. He dried her carefully, lingering over her breasts, kissing her again and again. She shuddered as arousal wrapped them both in a veil of need.

Carter rifled through his suitcase for protection and joined her on the big bed. He leaned over on one elbow, curling his hand in her ponytail and holding her down. "You're mine tonight, Abby."

The slight tug at her scalp made her breath come faster. He was showing her an edge to their passion that they had only skated near before. She craved his forcefulness and would give him everything in return.

When he kissed her once more, she sank her teeth

into his bottom lip. "I want to push you over the edge, cowboy. What do you think of that?"

His cheekbones flushed dark red, and his pupils dilated. "I think you talk too damn much." His lips and teeth and tongue dueled with hers, establishing dominance, but with a dollop of tenderness that promised safety in a storm.

When he entered her with a guttural groan, she felt the sting of tears. Maybe love didn't come so quickly. But who was to say? What she felt for Carter was an overwhelming tide, a thrilling rush of passion. She *loved* him. Or she was *falling* in love with him. What did semantics matter when the ending of their story was so painfully clear?

He took her long and hard and then soft and slow, drawing out the pleasure until she was wild with wanting him, her fingernails marking his powerful shoulders.

"Carter…" She cried out his name when she came, lost to reason, lost in a lover's embrace.

She felt the moment when his control snapped and he let his own passion overcome him. Holding him as tightly as she could, her body absorbed the aftershocks. Her fingers tousled his hair, and her breath mingled with his.

Gradually, their heartbeats slowed. The sweat dried on their bodies.

Carter mumbled something inaudible and reached to pull up the covers.

In seconds, they were both asleep.

* * *

Abby awoke hours later, disoriented and confused. The bedroom was strange. But awareness gradually returned, and she knew whose big warm body was entwined with hers.

It was 5:00 a.m. She slipped carefully out from under the masculine arm and leg that held her pinned to the mattress. Carter never moved.

With the flashlight on her phone, Abby found clothes in her suitcase and put them on. Cotton pants with a drawstring waist, comfortable, but thick enough to protect her legs if she had to kneel on the ground. A long-sleeve T-shirt to guard against a cool morning breeze. Canvas sneakers that had seen better days.

The whole process took less than five minutes. She decided to let Carter sleep. After all, he had to drive them back to Royal later today. They'd brought no provisions for breakfast. That was an oversight. But she kept energy bars in her camera bag for just such an occasion.

She made it all the way through the house and out to the driveway before she remembered that she needed the keys to Carter's car.

Muttering under her breath, she stowed her gear in the trunk and returned to the house, stubbing her toe on a loose brick at the edge of the driveway as she moved in the dark. When she reached the top step, the door opened, and there he was, filling the space.

"Are you trying to ditch me, Abs?"

The slight hint of annoyance in his voice could have meant anything.

"No," she said. "But you were dead to the world. And you have to drive this afternoon. I'm used to being on my own."

"I'm sure you are."

Now there was no mistaking his displeasure. "Come on," he said. "I have the keys. I assume we're headed to the festival site?"

She exhaled. "Yes."

They didn't speak on the way across the island. Abby asked him to stop a time or two for a quick shot. But what she needed most, with her back to the east, was to see the sunrise bathe the upcoming Soiree on the Bay with mystical light.

The weather was perfect. Only a few high thin clouds to add punctuation to the story she was hoping to capture. Already, she could hear the commentary.

Thousands of festivalgoers will soon descend on Appaloosa Island, eager to eat and drink and rock out to the sounds of America's popular bands. But do they realize what beauty blossoms here in the sounds of silence?

Carter interrupted her mental flight of fancy. "Where do you want me to park?"

"Closer to the water, please. And you don't have to get out. I'll be ranging around."

His silence lasted two breaths, then three. "I'll go with you, Abby. I'm sure you don't need me, but it will make me feel better."

"Fine." She grabbed her camera and set up the tripod.

After filming a loop of the stars cartwheeling across the heavens, she focused on the ribbon of dawn at the horizon. When she was satisfied, she put the tripod back in the trunk and shouldered the camera. "Let's go."

They walked the festival grounds for the next half hour, shooting empty stages gilded in light. Focusing on sawdust paths and eventually, beams of sunlight traveling across the water. The work was exacting and exhilarating in equal measure.

She had assumed she would feel self-conscious having Carter at her heels. But his presence was oddly comforting. She was used to being on her own, that was true. Still, he added something to her routine, something indefinable and wonderful.

By the time the sun was fully up and beginning to warm the moist air, Abby was starving. Carter still hadn't said much. He was wearing his clothes from last night as if he had dashed out of the house to catch her and not bothered with his suitcase.

"Thank you," she said stiffly. "It was nice having company."

He ruffled her hair. "You're welcome." A huge yawn seemed to take him by surprise. "Is it nap time yet?"

"I was hoping you could summon a fast-food place out of thin air. I'd kill for coffee and a bagel."

He slid into the driver's seat and turned on the AC. It was amazing how quickly the Texas heat multiplied. "I can do better than that," he said. "I asked my buddy to arrange for a few supplies in the kitchen. According to him, a local lady cooks for them and delivers whenever they request meals."

"Great setup!" Abby exclaimed. "Does this car go any faster?"

Back at the house, they found a container of home-made blueberry muffins on the counter and in the fridge, fresh-squeezed orange juice along with a sausage and egg casserole. The coffeepot soon produced a heavenly aroma.

They ate at the island, standing up.

Carter reached over to brush a crumb from her chin. "Not to be sexist," he said, "but I'm astounded how beautiful you look at this hour of the morning. You're the opposite of high-maintenance, aren't you?"

She put her hands to hair that was riotously out of control, because she had gone to bed with it wet. "I appreciate the compliment, but I'm going to need to seriously up my game before tonight. Would you mind if we headed on back to Royal?"

He stared at her even as she kept her gaze on her breakfast. "No morning *exercise*?" he drawled, his meaning impossible to misinterpret.

Her cheeks burned. What could it hurt? One last time? Of course, that's what she had told herself about last night. "Sure," she said, hoping the word was breezy and not filled with indecision. "It's still early."

He picked her up and tossed her over his shoulder, making her squeal with laughter. "What are you doing, Carter?" she said breathlessly.

His answer was succinct. "Saving time."

She thought he might suggest a shared shower. But no. Instead, he stripped her naked, undressed himself and bent her over the arm of the settee, taking her from behind.

He did pause at the last second to grab a condom, but after that, things got a little crazy. It almost seemed as if was trying to prove a point or maybe coax her into protesting.

Not a chance. She memorized every frenzied thrust, every touch of his hands on her body. Her heart was breaking, even as she climaxed sharply with his weight pressing her into the soft upholstery.

When it was over, he tugged her to her feet, cupped her neck in two hands and kissed her lazily. "Now *that's* the way to start a morning," he said.

Fourteen

Carter was sleepy on the way back to Royal. Abby had been right about that. And as soon as they left the ferry and made it over onto the highway, she was out cold, her neck bent toward the window at an awkward angle.

It was just as well. Carter needed time to think. He and Madeline had tumbled into a relationship based on sex, and that had ended in disaster. Was he doing the same thing with Abby? He honestly didn't think so. What he felt for her was different, not even in the same ballpark.

After Madeline walked out on him, he had been furious, but he had repaired his life and carried on.

If Abby left for good, he feared there would be a gaping hole in his chest, his world, his *heart*. He was in danger of loving her—or maybe he already did, but it was too soon to admit it. How could he let her go?

Could he persuade her to stay in Royal? Surely, she understood what bound him to Texas. The responsibilities he carried, the weight of his heritage and his family's expectations. But would it matter in the end?

She roused about two hours into the trip and reached instantly for one of the insulated flasks of coffee. After a long drink, she smoothed her hair and rubbed her eyes. "Sorry," she muttered. "You want me to drive now?"

"I'm fine." He squeezed her hand briefly. "Abby?" His heart pounded. "Have you thought about maybe staying in Royal longer than you first planned? You could move in with me until the festival is over and even after that. I have plenty of room to set up a studio for you."

Her silence echoed inside the car. It lasted for ten seconds. Or fifteen. Maybe an eternity. She had gone still as a bunny rabbit caught in headlights. "Well, I…"

The leaden weight of disappointment settled in his gut. "You don't have to decide right now. Just think about it."

He was glad that controlling the car gave him an excuse not to look at her.

Abby kicked off her shoes and curled her legs beneath her. She sighed. "I would love to stay longer, Carter, I really would. But as soon as the festival is over, my father has blocked off some time to help me with editing and postproduction of my documentary. And that will be in California."

He knew it was time to change the subject. "So have you settled on an angle for the film? A theme?"

Again, he experienced that unsettling lag between his seemingly benign question and her response. Abby tapped her fingers on the armrest. "I have. Dad and I looked at some of my early footage. I talked it over with him. He thinks the missing money angle could be a hard-hitting hook. Possibly even make my project more commercial."

"Abby, no. You're getting into something that could be dangerous."

"Who would hurt me, Carter?" There was a little snap in her voice.

"Money makes people do strange things. Besides, I think you're way off base. Nobody on the festival advisory board *needs* money. Billy Holmes is rich. You saw the evidence of that. The Edmond kids are each loaded, not even taking into account what they'll inherit from their father one day. I truly believe the whole missing money thing is nothing more than gossip, despite what Billy said. It's probably a few hundred bucks."

"Pull over, please," Abby said, her voice tight.

He swung the wheel immediately, steering them into a state rest area. They both got out and faced each other over the top of the car.

Abby's gaze was stormy. "You don't have any respect at all for my professional integrity, do you?"

"Of course I do, but you're—"

She made a chopping motion with her hand, cutting him off. "No. You don't. You think of this documentary as *Abby's little hobby.* I may be young, Carter, but I'm neither immature nor foolish. I have goals and dreams. Which is more than I can say for you."

His temper lit. "You don't know me. Don't pretend like you do. Sunset Acres is *my* ranch now, not my parents'. It's a huge part of who I am."

"Ah, yes. A Texas rancher. An esteemed member of the Texas Cattleman's Club. There's more to life than cattle, Carter. Maybe that's why your precious Madeline left you."

Though the flash of regret on Abby's face said she regretted her harsh words, Carter sucked in a deep breath and counted to ten. They were both exhausted, and if he read the situation correctly, they were each fighting an attraction that was bound to hurt them both. Why keep pushing?

His fists were clenched on the roof of the car. He relaxed them and stepped back. "Do you need to use the restroom?"

Abby glanced at the squatty brick building baking under the afternoon sun. "Yes. I'll make it quick."

Carter didn't move. As he waited for her to return, he tried to find a way out. But every idea he pursued mentally ended up a dead end.

Besides, he had no proof that Abby was as caught up in him as he was in her.

As she walked across the sidewalk in his direction, he studied her as a stranger would. Her graceful long legs covered the distance quickly.

When she slid into the passenger seat and closed her door, he got in, as well. Thankfully, he had left the engine running. The day was hot as hell. It might set a record.

He rested one arm on the steering wheel, tasting defeat. "I don't want to fight with you, Abs. Especially with so little time left. Maybe we should call a truce."

She half turned in her seat, her expression heartbreaking. "Yes," she said. "My father told me something recently that resonated. He said some people come into our lives for a season. I think that's you and me, Carter. As much as we l…like each other, there's no future in it."

She stumbled over the word *like*. Had there been another word on her tongue? Had Abby been considering *love*?

He turned the radio on, covering the awkwardness. The last thirty minutes of the trip felt like an eternity. At the hotel, he got out to help Abby with her bags. Although she protested, he carried the two heaviest items upstairs, waited while she unlocked the door and then dumped everything on the extra bed.

She shifted from one foot to the other. "You can skip the reception tonight. I'm fine on my own."

Her words seemed prophetic. She didn't need him. "No back-sies," he said, hoping his smile was more genuine than it felt. "You invited me, and I said yes. What time should I pick you up?"

"Six thirty will work. Remember, it's black tie."

"Got it."

They stared at each other across what seemed like an acre of thick carpet. Her bed was mere steps away. He wanted her with a raw ache that didn't let up.

Abby was visibly nervous. Did she want him gone? Was that it?

"I should go," he said, hoping she would try to change his mind.

She nodded. "I'll see you at six thirty."

He carried the memory of her with him as he said a terse goodbye and made his way back downstairs. A woman of secrets, a woman of mystery. What thoughts raced behind those dark brown eyes?

He crashed hard when he got back to the ranch. The way he counted it, he'd barely managed four hours of sleep last night. Weaving on his feet, he knocked the AC down a few degrees and climbed into bed. But the hell of it was, Abby had taken up residence in that bed. He couldn't forget the taste of her skin, or the faint scent that was uniquely hers.

When he awoke, it was almost five. He scrounged in the fridge and found a couple of chicken legs and some potato salad. Standing in the kitchen wearing nothing but his boxers, he pondered his options. At the end of the party tonight, he could take Abby somewhere private. The Bellamy had lots of luxurious nooks and crannies. He could find a spot and lay out his argument.

The two of them had something. Sexual chemistry. And feelings. Strong feelings. If he admitted that to her and asked her to stay for him, for *them*, he figured there was a fifty-fifty chance Abby would agree.

Later, when he strode into the lobby of her hotel right on time, she was waiting for him. Was that by design? To keep him out of her room?

He was so caught up in analyzing her motives, it took him a few seconds to register what she was wearing.

When he did absorb the full picture, all he could do was shake his head. "Wow. You look incredible."

"Thank you," she said, her smile guarded.

Gone was the young woman who didn't mind getting dirty in pursuit of her career. In her place was a female who would draw the eye of every man at the Bellamy tonight. Abby's beautiful, wavy dark hair fell down around her shoulders. Her dress was red. *Sin* red. Fire-engine red. If his physical response to her had a color, it would be exactly this shade of red.

The dress was made of a thin, silky fabric in several layers that shifted and moved, drawing attention to her tall, alluring body. Tiny spaghetti straps supported a bodice that plunged deeply in front.

Abby's breasts curved in that opening, suggesting lush, unapologetic femininity. The dress clung to her form, defining her narrow waist and hugging her hips. The floor-length hem swished as she moved, revealing silver stiletto sandals and toenails painted to match the dress. The only jewelry Abby wore was a pair of dangly crystal and silver earrings.

Carter struggled to find his breath. "I should have taken you to a party sooner," he said, only half kidding.

She kissed his cheek casually. "*I'm* taking you, cowboy. You're my plus-one…remember?"

"I stand corrected." Outside, he helped her into the car and carefully tucked her skirt out of the way. When he slid behind the wheel, he shot her a glance. "If you were hoping to keep a low profile while you investigate possible fraud, that dress isn't going to do it."

She shrugged, toying with the small beaded purse in her lap. "I've decided not to discuss business with you anymore. It only makes us quarrel."

His lips twitched. "Understood. We're keeping things personal." He reached for her arm and rested his thumb where a pulse beat at the back of her wrist. She seemed so fragile, and yet he knew differently. Abby Carmichael was strong and resilient.

She tugged away, folding her hands primly in her lap. "Behave, Carter. I need to focus tonight."

"Is it possible you're a little obsessed with this movie you're doing? If you'd relax, we could eat and dance and mingle. You know…fun, normal people stuff."

"Don't pick a fight with me," she said. "I'll dance with you. But I'm also going to network the heck out of this party."

Abby realized that she wasn't at all bothered by Carter's gibes. She sensed the two of them were sustaining a fake argument for no other reason than to keep from jumping each other's bones.

The man was seriously hot. As a rich, rugged rancher, he always looked sexy, but tonight in his tux, he could make a girl swoon. His aftershave alone made her dizzy.

When they entered the Bellamy and headed for the ballroom where the Soiree on the Bay event was taking place, the whole place hummed with excitement. At a long table just outside the ballroom entrance, Abby surrendered her invitation.

No one was wearing name tags. This was too fancy a party for that. Besides, almost everyone present was a resident of Royal. They all knew each other.

Abby tucked her tiny purse in Carter's jacket pocket. As they made their way around the outer edge of the room toward the hors d'oeuvres, she spotted a number of people she recognized. The charismatic Rusty Edmond held court in one corner of the room, surrounded by beautiful women. He'd been married four times, but was currently single, hence the crowd.

All of the Edmond offspring were in attendance, though none of them were in the same vicinity. Ross was with his fiancée, Charlotte. Asher was deep in conversation with a cluster of men who all held cocktails and ignored the crowd that ebbed and flowed around them. Gina flitted from group to group, talking up the festival and laughing with friends.

Billy Holmes stood off by himself, surveying the chaos with a pleased smile.

Then suddenly, there was Lila Jones wearing a lavender gown that flattered her pale complexion. She flashed a smile at Carter and Abby. "Hey, you two. I want you to meet my fiancé, Zachary. Zach, this is Abby Carmichael, who's doing the documentary, and Carter Crane owns the Sunset Acres ranch just outside of town."

After greetings were exchanged, Abby whistled inwardly. Sweet little Lila Jones had hooked up with a blond, gorgeous guy like this? Good for her.

When someone else demanded Lila's and Zach's attention, Carter leaned down and whispered in Abby's ear, "Quit drooling. He's taken."

She grinned. "I can appreciate a fine work of art."

Carter brushed a strand of hair from her cheek and gave her an intimate smile, his body close to hers in the press of the crowd. "Is he your type? Blond and hunky?"

"I think you know that's not true." She searched his gaze. But it was as opaque and unreadable as the ocean at night. What was he thinking?

A few moments later, Carter was drawn into a conversation with a trio of fellow ranchers, something about alarm over the falling price of beef.

Abby was happy to escape that discussion. She finally made it to the food table and snagged a couple of shrimp and a bacon-wrapped scallop. Though this was cattle country, there wasn't much beef on the spread—only a tray of candied beef jerky.

The room was sweltering. Her forehead was damp. She spotted Valencia Donovan on the opposite side of the floor. Abby made her way through the throng. "Hey, Valencia. How are you?"

Valencia fanned her face with a napkin. "Hot. And you?"

"The same. I realized after I left you the other day that I had one more question I wanted to ask."

"Go for it," the other woman said.

"After your proposal was approved, who has been your contact on the committee? Who will be the one to disburse the funds to you?"

"Ah, yes. That would be Asher Edmond. He's been so helpful along the way. And very encouraging about how soon I might have the money. I owe him and the committee a great deal."

Before Abby could respond, another guest snagged Valencia's attention. Abby was alone for the moment. She wished fervently that she had thought to bring her video camera. Shots of this event, even if she only used snippets, would have been helpful. But in any case, she didn't have permission, so maybe it was a moot point.

Gradually, the room filled with glitz and glamour and excited chatter. The tuxedo-clad men were foils for the fashionable female plumage. Abby had grown up in an elite cross section of New York society. Her mother's family had deep connections in the city.

But here, she didn't belong. Just as she had never completely belonged back at home. The ache in her chest made her wonder if she would ever feel comfortable anywhere. Or maybe her destiny was to be what the Greeks referred to as *planetes*, wanderers.

Carter's life was anchored by the ranch. He had a purpose, a fixed spot in the universe.

Abby was a planet, always orbiting. Never finding home.

Suddenly, a large hand landed on her shoulder. She flinched and backed away instinctively. When she spun around, Billy Holmes stared at her.

"We need to talk," he said.

Was she imagining a hint of menace in his words? "Why?" she asked.

"I don't think I stressed enough how much I want you to drop the missing money idea. As I said before, it's a family matter. We're dealing with it. The festival doesn't need any bad publicity. Back off, Abby."

Before she could respond to his extraordinary remarks, Carter was back at her side. Scowling. He glared at Billy. "I hope I didn't hear you threatening my date."

Billy shrugged. "She's been poking her nose in a lot of places. If I were you, I'd convince her to stick to sweet stories with happy endings. Nothing like a libel charge to ruin a budding filmmaker's career."

Abby was stunned. This was a very different man than the one who had entertained her at his home. "But is it true?" she asked. "Is some of the money gone?"

Carter took her by the arm and steered her away. He vibrated with fury. "My God, you can't let it go! There are a dozen people in this room who would be happy to give you something for your documentary, but you keep beating a dead horse. Billy Holmes can ruin you in this town. I think it would be best if you go back to New York until the festival starts."

Abby felt as though someone had punched her in the stomach. There was not enough oxygen to breathe. "I was just doing my job," she whispered, conscious of eyes watching them.

"No," Carter said. "You were endangering your health and your reputation. *If* there is a significant amount of money missing—and I'm not saying there is—then all hell will break loose when the truth comes out. If Billy knows who the culprit is and he's protecting someone, you need to stay far, far away from this story."

"It's not your call," she hissed, angry and hurt.

"Maybe not. But I won't stand by and let you get caught in the cross fire. Come on," he said. "The band is starting to play."

The last thing Abby wanted to do was dance with

the infuriating, dictatorial Carter Crane. But short of making a scene, she had little choice.

He pulled her into his arms and held her close. The music and the other dancers swirled around them. Abby felt her heart break clean through when she laid her cheek against Carter's shoulder and finally admitted to herself that she was deeply in love with him.

His body was big and hard and warm against hers. When they moved too quickly, her skirt tangled with his legs, binding them close. She felt the steady beat of his heart, heard the ragged tenor of his breath. He smelled of orange and clove and soap.

For a moment, she debated telling him how she felt. Offering to move to Royal permanently. After all, he had broached the subject, at least on a temporary basis. A few weeks ago, such an idea would have been laughable. But that was before she met the man who made her want to put down roots. Royal might not feel like home, but Carter did.

Even when he was being an overbearing pain in the ass, she knew he was the man for her, the man she wanted. But it was so quick. Could such intense feelings be trusted?

Carter had already suffered through one broken relationship. He wouldn't be eager to rush into another. She knew he had feelings for her. Lust. Affection. But anything more? How could she take that gamble?

And what about her life and her career? Why did it always have to be the woman who made all the sacrifices? Again, she understood bleakly that she and Carter were the worst matchup imaginable.

When the band took a break, Gina Edmond spoke briefly. As did her brother and stepbrother and Billy Holmes. Rusty Edmond looked on with a proud smile, but didn't involve himself in the speeches.

At last, the formalities were over.

Despite how much she wanted to trust that what they had was worth fighting for, Abby couldn't get over the fact that Carter had said he wanted her to leave town. Which meant he couldn't be as emotionally involved as she was if he could so easily say goodbye. If she was looking for a sign, she had found one.

Her chest hurt so badly she wondered if she was having a heart attack. She reached in Carter's jacket pocket for her small clutch purse. "I'm leaving," she said brokenly. "I—I don't want to see you anymore. Goodbye, Carter."

His face went blank with shock. Before he could say anything, Rusty Edmond took him by the arm, demanding his attention. Abby used Carter's momentary distraction to flee. She was counting on the fact that it would take him a few moments to break free.

Thankfully, she found a Lyft driver waiting at the front entrance. She flagged him down, climbed in and gave the hotel address.

But she didn't cry until she was in her room with the door locked and the dead bolt turned.

Carter felt like he was living in an alternate universe. How could Abby simply disappear? They'd been having a fight, sure, but he thought their dance had smoothed over the rough patch. He loved holding her, moving to the music.

I don't want to see you anymore. Goodbye, Carter. It was only when he heard those words that the blinders had fallen. Yes, it was quick. And yes, such emotion was suspect. But dammit, he loved Abby Carmichael.

If he'd had doubts about that, the sick feeling in his gut spelled out the truth. He had held something fragile and beautiful in his grasp, but he had let it slip away.

For three hours he called her cell, and then the hotel room landline. Eventually, he resorted to storming the Miramar and banging on Abby's door. When the night manager politely asked that he leave, Carter drove to the ranch, momentarily defeated, but not deterred. He paced the floor until 3:00 a.m. After that, he finally slept.

The following morning was Sunday. There was nothing he *had* to do. Nothing but find Abby and tell her the truth. He loved her.

But as it turned out, he had missed his chance. She was gone. Checked out of the hotel. And he'd been the one to send her away. In fact, he had *told* her to go. He was an idiot.

His first instinct was to jump on a plane and follow her, but to what end?

The two of them had been dancing around an ugly truth for days. They had no common ground. Even so, he was a stubborn son of a bitch. He was passionate about Abby, and he refused to believe that love wasn't enough…all evidence to the contrary.

* * *

Abby returned to New York with her heart and her composure in shreds. To make matters worse, her mother was already staying at *Bradley's*. When she heard that Abby was home, she offered to come back to the apartment. But Abby declined, keeping her voice light and cheerful.

Life would go on.

The worst part was, she *had* to go back to Royal to film the festival. That was nonnegotiable. Otherwise, all the work she had done already would be wasted.

For five days, she huddled in her bed, crying, staring bleakly at the ceiling. How did anyone survive this kind of heartbreak? Carter was all she thought about.

Eventually, she got angry with herself. There was more to life than sex and love. She would go back to being the same person she had always been.

She showered and dressed and went to a museum. Had lunch at her favorite café. But it didn't help much at all. She *wasn't* the same person. Carter had changed her. He had made her want things. And she didn't know what to do.

Though she stayed out most of the day, there were no answers to be found. Late in the afternoon, she wandered into Central Park and walked the paths aimlessly. It was cloudy. A front had come through, bringing cooler temperatures and a smattering of raindrops.

A few things were clear. First, she had to return to the scene of her heartbreak. Even if she managed to avoid seeing Carter, the journey would be painful.

Second, she *would* finish her documentary. Either

with or without the stolen money angle, she would do her very best work, and she would be proud of it.

And last, she had to find some closure. Did that mean confessing her love and watching Carter squirm as he searched for a way to let her down easily? The prospect was depressing. Even if she offered to move to Royal, she didn't think he loved her. How could he? They had been together such a short time.

When her legs were rubbery with exhaustion, she found a bench and sat down to watch children playing kickball on a grassy slope. All around her, the world kept marching on. Even her mother had found love.

Abby sipped her iced coffee and tried to find meaning in her rather colossal personal failure. Was she supposed to learn something from this experience? And if so, what?

People passed her occasionally, following the path. One stopped. "Abby…"

That single word, uttered in a deep masculine voice…

"Carter?" She looked up at him, wondering if she was hallucinating.

When he sat down beside her, the warmth and solidity of his presence convinced her he was real. "I've been looking for you for hours," he said, his tone terse.

She refused to apologize. "You're the one who told me to leave Royal," she said. If the words were snippy, she couldn't be blamed.

He sighed mightily. "You can't possibly know how much I regret that."

The silence between them stretched painfully. Everything she wanted was at her fingertips. But she didn't know how to reach for it…didn't know how to be true to herself and avoid her parents' mistakes.

Carter looked as handsome as ever, although perhaps there were new lines on his face, new shadows in his beautiful blue eyes. She didn't want to make him unhappy. Heck, she didn't want to make herself unhappy.

Did he expect to pull a ring out of his pocket and have her fall into his arms? Or maybe she was assuming too much. He might be here for nothing more than a booty call.

Suddenly, it was more than she could bear. She sprang to her feet. "You shouldn't have come," she said. Despair roiled inside her. She'd spent almost a week trying to forget him. How dare he stir things up all over again? It wasn't fair.

Carter reached out and took her wrist, his fingers warm as they curled against her skin. "I had to come, Abby. We weren't finished."

"Oh, yes," she said. "We were." But she couldn't find the strength to pull away from him. "There's no solution, Carter." That was the hell of it. "I can't see a way forward. Unless I give up everything. And even then, it would be on the off chance that we might end up with more than a hot and crazy affair."

"Oh, Abs." He closed his eyes and bowed his head, his posture defeated. After long, confusing seconds, he straightened and made her sit down again. He angled his body, so she could see his face. "I love you, sweet woman. And yes, it's for real. I struggled as much as you did. We were both struck by lightning, weren't we?

And it left us reeling. But even if it was quick, it wasn't fake. We have to get used to that idea, maybe. But I have time, if you do."

"I don't understand." She was afraid, too afraid to be crushed a second time.

Carter looked as if he had aged in a week. He was haggard, with dark circles beneath his eyes. The handsome cowboy was still there, but he was rough around the edges.

Now he took both of her hands. "I have never felt for any woman what I feel for you, Abby. It's as if we swapped hearts, and yours is beating inside me. When I first saw you that night, I thought you were beautiful and mysterious, and I wanted to know more. By the time we left the bar at the Miramar, you had already staked a claim."

"Love doesn't happen that fast," she whispered.

"Maybe it does." His smile was curiously sweet. "I'm thirty-four years old, Abby. I've made my share of mistakes. But I don't want this to be one of them. Tell me, Abs. Am I on my own here?"

For the first time, she saw the vulnerability deep in his blue-eyed gaze. She found her voice. "I love you, too, Carter. How could I not?"

But even then, her stomach clenched. Love wasn't the problem.

He folded her close against his chest. They had skated perilously close to disaster. He stroked her hair. "You're my heart. I'm sorry I hurt you. That was the last thing I wanted."

In his arms, she was safe. Secure. Loved. But still

she felt shaky. There were questions. And hurdles. Did she have the courage to bet all her cards on this one man? What if she gave up everything, and the two of them didn't last? "I'll have to figure a few things out," she said. "But I'll do it."

Carter pulled away, his chiseled jaw hard. "No. This is all on me. And I've already put things in motion."

"In motion?" She frowned at him.

He shrugged. "I've spoken to my family. Told them I'm in love with you. And I've made it clear that Sunset Acres will no longer be my first priority."

She blinked, stunned. "What does that even mean?" Was he proposing a long-distance relationship?

Carter's eyes seemed to be sending her a message, but she was puzzled. "I'll still hold the reins if they want me to," he said. "But we're hiring a manager. My parents and my sister agreed once they understood my position. I'll still have to spend a few days in Royal once a month, but other than that, I'm yours. We'll travel the world, or you can show me New York. Whatever you want."

She put her hands to her cheeks. "But that ranch is you, Carter. You love it."

He shook his head slowly. His gaze locked on hers as if he was willing her to believe. "It's just some cows and dirt. *You*, Abby. It's you I love."

Tears leaked from her eyes. The enormity of what he was saying overwhelmed her. How could a man walk away from a legacy?

He reached in his pocket. First, he handed her an

expensive linen handkerchief. It was too pretty to get wet, but she wiped her face anyway.

Then Carter held out a box. "I went to Harry Winston before I came to find you. That was probably a mistake. I realize that now. I should have let you choose. But I wanted to give you a ring, so you would know I'm serious. We can exchange it."

Was this really happening? In a situation that was impossible, had Carter actually found a way?

Abby flipped the lid. She stopped breathing for a full three seconds. "Oh, Carter." He had bought her an enormous, flawless emerald. The setting was extremely plain, so there was nothing to detract from the magnificence of the stone. It would have cost him a fortune, even by Royal standards.

When she didn't move, he tried to take it back. "You'd rather have a diamond, wouldn't you?"

The dismay on his face galvanized her. She smacked his hand away. When she pulled the ring from the box, a ray of sunlight peeked from behind the clouds, struck the stone and flashed emerald fire in a million directions. She stared at the stone in awe. "Put it on me, please."

Gently, Carter slid the ring onto her left hand. "Marry me, Abby. When the engagement has been long enough. When you're sure."

Her heart quivered with relief and hope and love. "I'm sure, Carter." She cupped his face in her hands. "Maybe you won't believe me, but I'm sure I want to live with you in Texas. Honestly, I do. All my life I've searched for a way to fit in. But then I met you, and I realized I had found home. It doesn't matter if I don't like cows, or I miss Broadway. When I'm with you, I have everything I want."

He shook his head slowly, his expression wary. "We'll talk about this. Marriage is about compromise, or so I've been told. We don't have to make any hard-and-fast decisions today."

She beamed at him. "But you already have. You were ready to give up your family's legacy. That means more to me than you'll ever know." A man who would do that wanted more than sex. He wanted forever, it seemed. The knowledge made her dizzy.

Carter kissed her forehead. "I want you to be happy, Abs. That's the most important thing, I swear. And I'll prove it to you."

"I believe you." She held out her hand and let the sun play with the emerald.

He tucked her in the crook of his arm. "The doorman told me your mother had moved out. And that you were living up there in that apartment all alone. Though he wouldn't give me any clue where to find you, so I'm not exactly on good terms with him."

"George is a sweetie. I'll vouch for you."

Her new fiancé kissed her hard, making her pulse race. "Does that mean I can stay for breakfast?" he asked, his hot gaze locking with hers, making her shiver.

"Oh, yes." Her body heated, already imagining the long night ahead.

They stood in unison, each ready to get on with their new life. Carter tucked his arm around her waist. "I love you, Abby."

"I love you, too."

He pulled back for a moment. "One more thing. I think you may have been right about the festival money. I'm sorry I tried to steer you away."

"Tell me."

He stared at her, started to speak and then kissed her forehead. "Can it wait until tomorrow? We're going to have to go back. But we can hash it out together. Okay?"

"You're really going to keep me in suspense?"

He lifted her hand to his lips and kissed the back of it. "This thing with you and me is brand-new, Abby. And we're here in this romantic city. Let's take one night just for us. Dinner and a show? What do you think?"

She searched his face and knew he was right. The festival secrets would keep. Tonight was a celebration. As she went up on her tiptoes and kissed him, his arms came around her and held her tight. "I love you," she whispered. "And if you don't mind, I think I'd rather spend the evening in bed. It seems like an eternity since we were together."

His eyes blazed with happiness and sexual intent. "I won't argue with that, Abs. Take me to your apartment and have your way with me."

"I thought you'd never ask…"

* * * * *

Don't miss the next book in
the Texas Cattleman's Club: Heir Apparent series:
Trapped with the Texan
by USA TODAY *bestselling author Joanne Rock*

#2815 TRAPPED WITH THE TEXAN

Texas Cattleman's Club: Heir Apparent • by Joanne Rock

To start her own horse rescue, Valencia Donovan needs the help of wealthy rancher Lorenzo Cortez-Williams. It's all business between them despite how handsome he is. But when they're forced to take shelter together during a tornado, there's no escaping the heat between them...

#2816 GOOD TWIN GONE COUNTRY

Dynasties: Beaumont Bay • by Jessica Lemmon

Straitlaced Hallie Banks is nothing like her superstar twin sister, Hannah. But she wants to break out of her shell. Country bad boy Gavin Sutherland is the one who can teach her how. But will one hot night turn into more than fun and games?

#2817 HOMECOMING HEARTBREAKER

Moonlight Ridge • by Joss Wood

Mack Holloway hasn't been home in years. Now he's back at his family's luxury resort to help out—and face the woman he left behind. Molly Haskell hasn't forgiven him, but they'll soon discover the line between hate and passion is very thin...

#2818 WHO'S THE BOSS NOW?

Titans of Tech • by Susannah Erwin

When tech tycoon Evan Fletcher finds Marguerite Delacroix breaking into his newly purchased winery, he doesn't turn her in—he offers her a job. As hard as they try to keep things professional, their chemistry is undeniable...until secrets about the winery change everything!

#2819 ONE MORE SECOND CHANCE

Blackwells of New York • by Nicki Night

A tropical destination wedding finds exes Carter Blackwell and maid of honor Phoenix Jones paired during the festivities. The charged tension between them soon turns romantic, but will the problems of their past get in the way of a second chance at forever?

#2820 PROMISES FROM A PLAYBOY

Switched! • by Andrea Laurence

After a plane crash on a secluded island leaves Finn Steele with amnesia, local resident Willow Bates gives him shelter. Sparks fly as they're secluded together, but will their connection be enough to weather the revelations of his wealthy playboy past?

SPECIAL EXCERPT FROM

⊕HARLEQUIN

DESIRE

*A tropical-destination wedding finds exes
Carter Blackwell and maid of honor Phoenix Jones
paired during the festivities. The charged tension
between them soon turns romantic, but will the
problems of their past get in the way of a second
chance at forever?*

Read on for a sneak peek at
One More Second Chance *by Nicki Night.*

"Listen." Carter broke the silence when they reached her door.
"I didn't mean to upset you."

Phoenix cut him off. "Don't worry about it."

"I thought the timing was right. We were getting along
and…"

"It's evident you still have an issue with timing," Phoenix
snapped.

Her comment stung. Carter took a deep breath and exhaled
slowly. He tried not to lose his patience with her.

"I'm sorry. I shouldn't have said that." Phoenix carefully
stepped over the threshold and turned back toward Carter.

"I'm sorry, too. Hopefully we can move on. It was nice
being friendly. Maybe one day we could go back to that."

Phoenix looked away. When she looked back at Carter, there
was something unreadable in her eyes. Had she been more
affected by his news than he realized? Their eyes locked. Carter
felt himself moving closer to her.

"We just need to get through the wedding tomorrow and the
next few days, and we can go back to living our normal lives.